Troika To Utopia

4.11.13

Troika To Utopia

A Docu-drama in Three-Quarter Time

Louis A. Coppola

authorHOUSE®

AuthorHouse™
1663 Liberty Drive
Bloomington, IN 47403
www.authorhouse.com
Phone: 1-800-839-8640

First published by AuthorHouse 07/28/2011

ISBN: 978-1-4634-3704-6 (sc)
ISBN: 978-1-4634-3703-9 (ebk)

Printed in the United States of America

This book is printed on acid-free paper.

Also by

Louis A. Coppola:

Essay-fiction Books

Homecrest Avenue, Silhouettes of an Accidental Family

C.B.S, The Chucklehead Broadcasting System

Plays

Chiarscuro

Troika To Utopia
(A Docu-drama In Three-Quarter Time)

Television

Checkmate, ABC/TV, The Benson Series

Last night I had a housekeeping dream
Odds and ends were discarded
Perhaps the final proofing stages,
From the trash I retrieved a hammer:

I go, we can't throw this away.
It's the symbol of Russia.

O, says Dima, in deep rolling Russian
More garbled and sensual than understood:

Vot vam molot, Vot vam cepn,
Eto nach cobetec uú zepõ,
Hoznech zhne, a cozemg cyú,
B cë pabuo poluzhesh xyú . . .
I give you hammer,
I give you sickle.
Symbol of Soviet Union.
Neither gives money
Only pennies.

Ψ

We no longer look for the Pax Romana, the imperial peace of Rome, nor simply the Pax Humana, peace among humans, but the Pax Gaeia, the peace of the earth and every being on earth. This is the original, final peace granted by whatever power brings our world into being. Within the universe, planet earth with all its wonder is the meeting place of the divine and the human. To tell the story of anything you have to tell the story of everything.

Thomas Berry, Genesis Farm,
Blairstown, NJ

CHARACTERS: PART ONE

Coachie, or Coachie, Nikita Sergeiyevnov, 50; tour guide; doubles as Judge, BG characters
Mamushka-Mother Russia, doubles as Mrs. Ulyanov and BG characters
Alexander "Sasha" Ulyanov; Lenin's brother
President-Judge Matryoni
Lenin or Vladimir Ilych Ulyanov, 40's
Nadya Krupskaya, his wife, 40's
Mrs. Ulyanov, late 20's; mother of Lenin and Sasha
Inessa Armand, 30's; Lenin's confidant
Zinoviev, Grigorii Eseyevich, 30's
Bogdanov, 30's
Lunacharsky, 30's
Maxim Gorky, 40
Marya, 30's; his wife;
Two servants, age 19; Gorky's theatre students
Tsar Nicholas (Nicky) Romanov, 40's
Tsarina Alexandra (Sonny), his wife; 30's
Natasha, 20's; cousin to Tsarina
Anna, 20's; a family friend
Rasputin, 30's; a lewd, dissolute monk with unusual powers
Fritz Platten, 30's; liaise Swiss socialist
General Ludendorf, 40's; of the German high command
Aide to Ludendorf, 20's
A Train Conductor

Conspirators: pro-monarchist noblemen

Prince Felix Yusupov, 30, cousin to Nicholas, Oxford educated playboy, patriotic, determined, objects to Rasputin's lascivious intrusion into government and the nobility, blames him for Russia's disasters.
Vladimir Pureshkevitch, 40's; a government minister; d 1920 of typhus in Novorossiysk; aristocrat, resolved conspirator, leader of early Russian fascism; Duma member; out to save the institution of the monarchy; leader of Right-Wing Party; anti-Bolshevik; joined White Army So. Russia (Shulgin, p480);
Boris, Grand Duke Dimitri Pavlovich, 26, b 1891, d 1942, bachelor, nephew of Alex III; ex-court minister
Dr. Vasily, 30's, sensitive, vacillator

Haunts and various BG characters

Music: waltzes in different tempi

PART 1

ACT ONE

Scene 1: Curbside of Le Bistro

Time: Post Stalin.
Place: A taxi area curbside of the Pearly Gates Bistro and sidewalk café.
Characters: Coachie; Mamushka; Haunts composed of formerly notable shakers and movers; Judge Matryoni; Sasha; and Lenin.

Open: MUSIC: distant, plaintive Emperor's Waltz played on organ grinder.)

Coachie: (To horses.) Dare I name names? Eh? What do you say? Names or no names? (Drinks from a bottle.) Name names n' our hides won't be worth a fig. We'll burn twice, yes, you, too, my Orlov beauties, on earth and in hell. Put to pasture all of us. I'll be chained to a park bench—Tfu! (Spits.)—And they'll boil your bones for soap. (Whinny.) Just thinking out loud. (Whinny.) You, too, eh? Why not? We all have rights. The right to a bit, harness and whip. Tfu! Nasdrovia! (Drinks.) Maybe just one or two names? (Whinnying.) None. Ok. Have an apple. (Horses balk; frightened.) Easy fellows. No wolves just shadows. Back to work, my dearies. An idle brain's the devil's playground. Like that? I don't. Tfu! (Dons cabbie hat.) What? Who calls? Who wants a ride? Here. Chew this. (Tosses apple at shadows.) Leave me in peace! (To passing public.) Ride, sir, m'am? Tfu! Here, my dearies. An apple a day keeps the haunts away, especially when laced with vodka. Here, my beauties, wet your lips. Apples n' vodka go far on a winter day. Yes, yes. Mm. The heart needs a jolt when it's cold n' it's always cold. Goddamn cold. Brr! Russians love vodka. It's the only thing that doesn't freeze. Like my little joke? I don't. The older I get the colder I get. (Puts on souvenir apron.) Tours! Notable taverns, famous graves marked n' unmarked. Sights n' frights! That's a twist. Like it, my beauties? I don't. The truth'd kill tourism n' topple the government, that corrupt—Sir, Madame, ride a gilded troika, wonder cab of a bygone Monarchy. Gone n' good riddance. Tfu! Map to the Tsars! Screw you, too. Russia wasn't built in a day. Heads had to roll. Free photos. Excellent quality: Stalin, Lenin, Trotsky, Rasputin, the Romanovs, a family portrait before and after. You get what you give. Coins, stamps, spoons, painted eggs, matryona, and the doll within the doll. If you pay y'ride, y'don't y'walk. Map to the Tsars, sir? Kolomenskoe, the old Tsarist estate, Ivan the Terrible lived there, Peter The Great spent his youth there sheltered from Streltsky revolt; St. Petersburg: Nevsky Prospect, Peter n' Paul, Tsarkoe Selo—the winter palace, the Hermitage, mass grave sights, homes of the old aristocracy—the Yusupov Palace where the nobles killed Rasputin. Away! Quiet! I tell you. Go back to hell! What am I saying? The hour is late. I've eaten one apple too many. But not to worry. We made our oats plus extra for a bottle. What? Another apple? You devils. Sightseeing! Photographs! Memorabilia! Relics old, new! Twenty kopeks a verst! Double for parties n' trysts. I break out livery; carriage lamp oil's expensive. Tour Moscow's Red Square named after centuries of blood staining the cobblestones. Guide, m'am? I'm bonded. Smell my breath. Old cow! Once there was a time—Well, all that's over and done. Now take me as I am, a guide, simple, retiring, unassuming, or don't. It's all the same to me, but a little business serves everybody. Taxi, sir? I mean, m'am? Shafts are gilded and etched. The middle bay sets the pace; the two outside horses keep their heads to the side to watch for wolves in all shapes and colors. Da. Tfu! Come! Ride my troika! You'll get more than you bargained for. Pick a lucky number. Get a free ride in the park. My bays're surefooted, strong. They know the way even in blinding snow. In the wind their tails flap and their manes fly like fire licking the sky. Look. My troika is antique guitar style with bronze mountings. Seating is tête-à-tête. When it's late and quiet and the ground is covered with snow, we move along like spirits between two worlds, the thud of the heavy-footed bays in the snow, the stillness is crisp, the stars mix with the tinkling of the sleigh bells on the harness. Poetry in motion. I'm no poet myself, but I feel things, yes, more than poets themselves. Good God! I did things without thinking. I had no choice. But in my heart I—Come! Ride! Hear the sleigh bells cut the stillness like tears falling from heaven. See Catherine's Palace in Pushkin; the Hermitage; Uglich; follow the Cossack's footsteps to Kiev's St. Sophia Cathedral, the monastery of the caves; Yaroslavl; Sevastopol; onion domes; cemeteries, mass gravesites. Book a day trip south of Moscow to the province of Tula see Tolstoy's house in Yasnaya Ployana, his tomb in the park unmarked, but I know where it is. Novodyevichy Cemetery and the Wall of Urns with Ashes, among the trees, bushes, and flowers the graves of Gogol, Chekhov, Mayakovsky, Rubenstein, Scriabin, Prokofiev, and Nadezha Allilyeva, wife of Stalin, suicide in 1931 to which Stalin said, How could she do that to me? Gorky's dacha where he died mysteriously. See beloved Moscow, Red Square, and Lubianka—an insurance company turned into a house of horrors with one policy, terminal life. Tour torture chambers—sadists half fare. Enjoy the cuisine: blini, pirozhki, caviar; learn to make varenyky while they pull out your toenails. See the Kremlin; Lenin's Mausoleum n' Stalin's memorial. At the moment Stalin's in disgrace while they decide on a new burial site. Some say the Church of St. Bartholomew, others Siberia under tons of permafrost so he'll never rise again. (Enter conjured haunts holding unlit lanterns: "Mamushka.") In the Bistro on the stove. (They melt away.) Haven't thought of Mamushka in a dog's age. How could I forget—

(Off crash of pots and pans; haunts return helter-skelter and exit followed by Mamushka swinging a broom.)

Mamushka: Idiots! You take me for a dishrag? Come home, wipe your dirty feet and then off to the races. My apron is no horn of plenty.

Coachie: Mamushka, babushka. It's me, your son, Ivan.

Mamushka: What's that, a clue? Every Russian's Ivan.

Coachie: Ivan Ivanovich Sergeiyevnov from Kalinovka, the Don Bass.

Mamushka: O, yes, the pipe metal fitter. Your father was a serf. He bathed twice in his life—when he was baptized and when he was washed for burial. What do you want, Ivan Ivanovich Sergeiyevnov of the Don Bass? Wait. Let me guess. *You want to go to heaven.*
Coachie: I just want to talk with you.
Mamushka: Same thing. Well, it's late in the game, Ivan. Every guilty man's his own hangman. Frankly, you're headed into the permafrost with Stalin. Your religion is the city. Pray to the concrete, to Lubianca, for salvation. *O, black bread and butter. Just a morsel, Ma-mushka.* Tfu! The cupboard's empty. Work the fields, break your back, plow, plant, cultivate, sun up to sundown, and then call my name. Go! Menshevik, Bolshevik, Social Revolutionary! Embrace the devil you pay the price.
Coachie: We made a mess of things.
Mamushka: The understatement of the century. You set the devil to scratching his head. Who's right? Left? Middle of right, left of middle. Conservative right, Conservative left.
Coachie: Left of left.
Mamushka: Right of right. Conservative liberal, Liberal Conservative.
Coachie: Socialist Democrat; Reactionary Socialist; Bundists; Kadets; Centrist; Revolutionary Democrat; Reds, Whites, Pinks; Opportunists!
Mamushka: Enough hogwash! A pathetic bunch: yakety-yacking night and day, while the devil laughed up his sleeve. With the dawn limp bodies spin round dizzy from hair splitting, a tempest in a tea pot, walking backwards, gaunt-eyed, tongues swollen from hunger, a dumb faced smugness edged by grins on clownish monkey faces; then followed evictions, signs posted in windows: "Room for rent: No Russians!"
Coachie: They were the brains of the new intelligentsia.
Mamushka: Ivan Ivanovich Sergeiyevnov from Kalinovka, what do you know of brains, eh, a deluded pipe metal fitter from the Don Bass? You Godless degenerates. There should've been a third Revolution. Tfu! It sickens me to death that I issued such rotters. I gave you the greatest land empire in the world. How do you repay me? I gave you Pushkin, Tolstoy, Dostoyevsky, Prokoviev,

Tchaikofsky, Ballet Russe, Stanislavsky, Chekhov, Turgeniev, Gorky, the Orlov horse, the troika, and how do you repay me? Tfu! You spit in my face. Go! I wash my hands of you. Go! Hide your ugly soul deep in the cellars of Lubianca with the devil.

Coachie: Mamushka, I beg you, forgive me.

Mamushka: Tell y'what. Let's play a game for paradise, Troika, you played it as a child. Only on this ride there'll be no pretend only truth.

Coachie: That's not Troika. That's Russian roulette.

Mamushka: History demands truth! Now, cook me a soup, cabbie man. Bake me a bread no fillers. Mark well your words. All depends on forthrightness, and then maybe, just maybe, you'll get to sit by the stove with Gogol and Chekhov. Eh? Nice, yes? Maybe even sit on the top shelf, occasionally, no promises. I've got chicken soup working, black bread—

Coachie: Wonderful, wonderful! Begging your pardon, and that of my lovely bays. This is the Villa Blaesus on Capri—

Mamushka: Lovely, I'm sure, but first Mamushka has to set the table. We go to Simbirsk.

Coachie: A sleepy place. Narcosis is more apt.

Mamushka: Da. Make with the spiel. I'll wait for my cue. Don't worry. I'll know it when I hear it. And don't be long in the tooth. (Disappears up.)

Coachie: This is Simbirsk, fifteen hundred miles from Moscow due east. A few famous people were born here, Kerensky, Lenin, but left as soon as they could walk. It's one of those places, y'see. We're all born somewhere. It's what you do afterward. Simbirsk, on the Volga, all kinds of houses, big, small, huts, lean-twos bunched and scattered along the hills and ravines some with balconies, sun-blinds, belvederes, topped by pigeon-houses, small wooden boxes for starlings; courtyards overgrown with grass. The people are a mix of Tartars, Mongols, and Chubash tribes. Here, alleys wind between fences and deserted streets with important names like Astrakhan and Moscow Street. There are bazaars with heaps of bast, salted dry fish, vats of tar and fancy kulatch bread; wide open gates to inns smelling of manure; and overlaying the city is the torpidity of peace and calm that sailors find at sea. In the shade of a fence a goat and chickens sleep, dogs lie in heaps on farms; here and there someone sticks his head out of a window, looks left, right, spits, Tfu! and disappears. Street voices echo for miles along with footsteps on wooden sidewalks. Below, the Volga flows in deep thought dotted with islands, banks and bushes; in the distance sandy, yellow mountains are crowned with a blue forest; a seagull flaps his wings, glides down, skims the water, flies up and circles as a kite drifts above the gardens. Simbirsk is a picture postcard of slumber and stagnation, an excellent antidote for insomnia. One look puts you to sleep. On the outside chance of meeting someone in the street they yawn broadly, "Oh, but we've nothing to do, absolutely nothing. Ho-hum," and lazily drift off, making you wonder if they ever existed, or *even if you yourself ever existed.*

(Mamushka as Mom with a suitcase.)

Mom: Excuse me, kind sir. Is your cab at liberty?

Coachie: Da. Best rates anywhere—Reasonable.—Includes hot tea n' vodka, if you're so inclined. Whereto?

Mom: St. Petersburg 1887.

Coachie: Street?

Mamushka: S.S. Peter and Paul.

Coachie: The fortress? O, such a dismal place for a kind lady. May I suggest the Caucasus for sea and sun?

Mom: I go to my son, a student-patriot. Won a gold medal in academics.

Coachie: You should be proud. I'll give you a student rate.

Mom: Have you discounts for student protestors?

Coachie: The government does. They discount 'em n' lock 'em up.

Mom: And if accused of attempted assassination—O, goodness!

Coachie: That's bad business. Who? You mean the—O, my! The Tsar? That's a capital offense. The gallows—(Mom swoons; he catches her.) Easy, m'am. Have a seat. Sip a little of this. (Takes out bottle. Horses whinny.) Quiet. You had yours. M'am, you ok? You said, "attempted". He failed, eh? Too bad. They'll send him to Siberia. It's nothing.

Mom: Not to a mother. I couldn't bare it.

Coachie: Chin up. He who foresees calamities suffers them twice.

Mom: Please, to St. Petersburg. My son needs me.
Coachie: Climb in. Get comfortable.
Mom: Comfortable? How can I? Impossible.
Coachie: My horses are swift. Fear no bandits. I eat 'em for breakfast. Pull up the bearskin. The wind has teeth when speeding along. In Petrograd it's likely—30c. They cover the statues in wooden boxes to keep them from cracking. Stand still too long in Pete they'll wrap you in a box.
Ha. Like my little joke? I don't. Tfu! A big city for such a little lady with a kind face. I wanted to go to school in Peter to finish my education, but God had other plans. Excuse the expression, if you're an atheist.
Mom: My son is a forthright young man.
Coachie: No doubt like his mother.
Mom: We abhor lies. But he's got his father's disposition and refuses to bend. If you have children you know it's important to bend.
Coachie: You said a mouthful. One bends to survive. I have two children by my second wife. The first couldn't bend, n' died from typhus.
Mom: Oh, I'm sorry.
Coachie: She was a bitch anyway. Still, I wished her no harm.
Mom: On y sois qui mal y pense, bad to the one who thinks bad. Right now I can't think. We haven't even begun and I am exhausted. I had seven children by Ulyanov.
Coachie: You have a right to be exhausted.
Mom: Five survived, but now my eldest—Oh, dear me! He's just eighteen, you know. Won lots of gold medals in school. Sometimes I wish . . .
Coachie: We'll talk on the way. Pete's more than a stone's throw.
Mom: My Sasha is a serious boy, even tempered on the surface, but obstinate underneath. Sometimes it's hard to know what he's thinking. I don't want to be inside his head, but as his mother, I'd feel a lot better—
Coachie: If you were. That's the truth. Sooner or later you let them go.

Mom: Had I known how he really felt, his personal predilections, maybe, but he took after his father, a school inspector, a silent man.

Coachie: My father was silent too except when he ate. He would bang the table, bellow, and tear at his food like a mad dog. Ha. It was always frightening. But like the old folk say, a body can get used to anything, even hanging if it hangs long enough.

Mom: O, that word.

Coachie: One day my father gave me a such a laugh. Ha! His head fell forward into the soup. Ha! I laughed until I realized he was dead, and then I cried. Tfu! Why? I don't know to this day.

Mom: We cry for ourselves. Do you mind? I'm tired and—

Coachie: Suit yourself, m'am, ah, Mrs. Ulyanov. On the way I may catch a few winks myself. The bays know the way even in a snowstorm. Onward into the night! Whither do you rush in such headlong flight? Ee-yah! The stars have seen much. They'll see even more. School inspector? That explains it. Inspectors are quiet, important people. Take themselves seriously. They must. They have to inspect. If they're not serious who will believe what they say about what they inspect? Imagine a buffoon inspecting something important like my troika. He walks around, gives a look here, there, at the wheels, the seats, and the samovar. Is it clean, any leaks? Looks up the horse's tale; looks in his mouth, does he brush his teeth; comb his hair; are his ears clean; and then, he looks at the driver and if you don't grease his palm you fail inspection. It's hard on children, especially boys. They have to look stern.

Mom: Even to their mothers?

Coachie: Most of all. They know instinctively they can't fool the old man. I couldn't fool my father, although he fooled me. I saw him go into the ground like a mole and when he came up he called my name, but I ran behind my mother. I didn't recognize him. He was black as night. What else could a peasant do? Farming meant leaving home, traveling with no guarantee.

Mom: My husband traveled a lot before he died, setting up schools here and there, away months at a time.

Coachie: How did he die? (Sound of gaveling.)

Mom: We were a close-knit family. At meals my children would set the table and Sasha, the eldest, would carry in the samovar, insisted on it, saying, it was his duty while father was away. Ha, ha.
Judge: (Gaveling.) Order in the court!
Mom: It was funny at first because Sasha was smaller than the samovar, which seemed to float in from the kitchen like a golden silvery ghost. Of course we didn't laugh out loud. It would've hurt his feelings. Sasha was sensitive. To his credit, no one assisted and he never faltered. Now he's grown up, a man, and . . . My husband died of cerebral hemorrhage.
Coachie: I went to the Engineering Institute in Moscow. It was full of a lot of hangers-on, near-do-wells, slackers and revolutionary types. I fixed more than a few of them, but then I dropped out to work . . . So, you are comfortable, yes? Good. Petrograd is not just around the corner. If you get bored you have your book. O, Heinrich Heine!
Mom: You know his work?
Coachie: No. Sounds German. Ah, undt in Germann! Buch der?
Mom: Lieder, Book of Songs. My son asked me to bring it.
Coachie: In German?
Mom: Sasha speaks three languages. I taught him French myself.
Coachie: What a lucky boy. My father spoke only one language. Violence. Let's get rolling. Maybe some stops on the way to rest the horses, take on a passenger or two, if you don't mind, to defray the overall expense. O, I remember. Heinrich Heine, poet German—Jewish. He's on the government list of forbidden books like Chernyshevsky's What Is To Be Done? Cost him 27 years in jail and exile; Plekhanov, Heine, the list is long. Eeyah! (Cracks whip; sings.) Ochi chernye, ochi cguchie y prekraznye y mo-guchie . . . (Dark eyes; hot and passionate. Gaveling.)

Scene 2: Courtroom

Mom: Recant, I beg you. Ask the Tsar for mercy. Your life will be spared. I have some assurance from a friend in high position. One of your associates pleaded for mercy and was spared. Do you hear me, Sasha?

Sasha: (Rising.) I am sorry, mother. Forgive me, but I can't, I won't beg for mercy. After all I vowed that would be playing the hypocrite. Mama, I want to die for my country.

Mom: What are you saying? I am your country, your mother. My son, why so severe? You were always carefree and joyful. You loved theatre, poetry, especially music. After your father died you became somber, would disappear before my eyes in deep thought, and I wasn't sure what it meant. I see now you took it to heart. Your father lived his life and would want you live yours, not throw it away on a terrorist dream.

Sasha: Mother, stop. I beg you to stop. I made up my mind. I die for you, for father, and for my country. I go to meet father whom I prize above all things of this world. When father died I died with him. The world was no longer the same. Mother, please, be proud that I stand up for liberty, human rights, freedom of speech, and not the lies of the monarchy. Try to understand. You didn't raise a liar for a son. Come what may. I will not lie. (Lenin appears in BG.)

Lenin: You are right, big brother. They are wrong. One day they will pay.

Sasha: Now I kiss you and the family goodbye. Tell them I love them and wish them all the happiness in the world.

Lenin: A revolutionary's obligation is to stay alive to fight another day.
Mom: Sasha . . .
Sasha: Do not cry for me, mother, cry for Russia.
Judge: Alexander Ilyaevitch "Sasha" Ulyanov, son of Ilya Nikolayevich and Maria Alexandrovna Ulyanov. (Sasha turns to Judge.) You have three sisters and two brothers: Olga, Maria, Anna, Dimitri, and Vladimir. Is that correct?
Sasha: Yes. (Lenin appears in BG.)
Judge: You are a student of Zoology at St. Petersburg University.
Sasha: Yes.
Judge: You won a university gold medal for your work in annelid worms. Congratulations. (Incredulously.) Despite your youth, eighteen years old, very impressive, you are already in your fourth year. Excellent. How did you support yourself?
Sasha: My father until his death. I tutored in mathematics, science—
Lenin: And chess. (Moves piece; Sasha smiles, counters.)
Judge: You are accused of an assignation against Tsar Alexander by explosives found on your person. You deny the charge?
(Lenin moves piece. Sasha counters.)
Sasha: No.
Judge: Regarding proclamations found on you—who hectographed them?
Sasha: I did.
Judge: Anyone else?
Sasha: Yes. But I refuse to give the name.
Judge: Some of your colleagues fled abroad. Why didn't you?
Sasha: I didn't want to. I wished to die for my country.
Judge: Who else took part in this abortive attempt?
Sasha: (Studying chess board.) No one.
Lenin: Everyone!
Sasha: I alone am guilty.
Lenin: They are the guilty ones.
Mother: Sasha, tell him. You were not alone.
Sasha: Your move, little brother.
Mom: Renounce your actions. Friends in high places promise to spare your life regardless of the verdict.

Sasha: Impossible. Checkmate. Mother, I cannot. It would mean going against all that I believe. I'd have to reveal names, details of the plot.
Mom: Do it for your mother.
Sasha: No. I am not sorry for my actions. My only sorrow is for you, mama. Forgive me. (Embraces her; to Judge.) May I address the court?
Mom: Tell the truth. Live, I beg you.
Lenin: Another round, Sash?
Judge: (Gaveling.) Silence in the court! (Aside.) You know what's coming, those of you who aren't asleep. It's the noble act of a martyr. Wonderful! Yes? What glory to die young for a principle. The Americans hung John Brown and he was right. The boy is right, too, yet—Well, it's not a matter of right or wrong. It's the iron fist of the establishment. The only truth is what serves the beast. Elected official, and bureaucrats we're all go-along buffoons and clowns. And all the people can do is cry: What's the joke? Are you folks serious? What's the joke? That life must resort to savagery to affirm what was stolen from it in the first place, God given human rights. Between you, me and the lamppost this is just the start, the underbelly of things to come. Madness countered by greater madness. Rest assured, the lad will hang to some for a fool, to others a martyr; and only his mother will call his name, and one other. (Turns to court.)
Lenin: Think, brother. Live to fight another day.
Mom: He's just a boy, your honor. Eighteen years old. Return him to his mother, I beg of you. I will resurrect the healthy human instincts he had always lived by. Mercy, mercy!
Lenin: Mother, stop. Sasha owes these court butchers nothing. They're a reprehensible extension of a monarchy based on *convoluted truth*.
Judge: (Gaveling.) Silence! (Aside.) We wouldn't recognize truth if it dropped on our heads like a bowl of cold borscht. Personally, I prefer stroganov with black bread. Truth and justice are bland, whereas, a good lie is entertainment. Toss in the gallows and it's a show, something the French understood very well. Jean Pierre de Guillotine lived in a village. While dicing vegetables in the kitchen he made the connection between lopping off carrot tops

n' people's heads, n' voila, le guillotine. Bet he never stuck his neck out for nobody. O, the executioner's art. Enter, the tumbrel hauling victims along the street to execution square to the beat of drums, n' cat calls from the ghoulish mob in eager anticipation of Le Moment when the blade dropped. Boom! Another carrot top for the gods! I prefer drawing and quartering. Pure sadism. If the sucker feints douse him with water n' salt his wounds. Crucifixion's ok. Two thousand years later Jesus remains the greatest show on earth, an amulet nailed to a cross. Ha. Even the instigating Pharisees n' Sadducees couldn't top that. Alexander Ulyanov you may address the court.

Sasha: *The facts speak for themselves. I don't deny them. My defense consists solely in the right to present my motives, to speak of the reasons which persuaded me of the absolute necessity to commit this crime. Since early youth I was dissatisfied with the social system, but only after studying social and economic sciences did this conviction of the abnormality of the existing system strengthen in me; and the vague dreams of freedom, equality and brotherhood took shape for me in the scientific forms of socialism. Marx was right. Under capitalism labor is alienation, external to the worker, not part of his essential self. In his work he doesn't affirm himself, and is discontented. He doesn't develop freely his personal gifts, but mortifies and ruins his mind. The worker feels out side his work. He is only at home when not at work. His labor is coerced, not voluntary. It's not the satisfaction of a need, but merely the means to satisfy external needs.* (Judge nods.) *When no physical or other compulsion exists such labor is shunned like the plague. Labor that alienates man is labor of self-sacrifice and mortification . . . and results in the horrible loss of himself as a unique entity. He becomes an alienated, mechanical creature with no moral compass. It is everyman's duty to emancipate himself from petty squires and philistines who abuse workers for egoistic ends.* (Judge yawns.) *There is only one correct path of development, that is the path of words and the press. Every social change is a result of change in consciousness of society. You yawn, and people yawn too. The difference is you are educated to know better. They are kept ignorant. But you share in common an indecent brainwashing. No matter how serious the subject if it's not* *straight forward A, B, C,—pictographic—it elicits that dull-eyed yawn. The enemy is complacency, and self-deception. So what do you do when those who supposedly represent you repeatedly spit in your face? Given the government's attitude to intellectual life, the scientific examination of questions is seriously impeded. The government is so powerful, the intelligentsia so weak and concentrated in a few cities, that government could deprive it of the only possibility: the last vestiges of freedom of speech. Convinced of the absolute subjective need of freedom of thought and expression, it was necessary to look into whether there exist in Russian society the elements on which a struggle for freedom could depend. Russian society differs from Western Europe: It is inferior intellectually, and we have no firmly united classes that might restrain the government. For an intellectual person, the right to think freely and to share his thoughts with those who are inferior to him in development is not only an inalienable right, but also even a necessity and duty.*

Judge: *You expound generalizations known to the court more or less. How did they affect you?*

Sasha: *This government destroys initiative in order to preserve its stranglehold on the people. You rob us of hope, kill our finest impulses, steal our dreams, and wonder why we rebel. The intelligentsia is so weak and disorganized, that it can't engage in open struggle. Only through terror can it defend its right to thought and intellectual participation in society. Terror is the form of struggle created by the 19th c. It is the only defense available to the minority, which is only strong in the spirit and conviction of its right to oppose the majority's oppression. Russian society exists in such circumstances that it is only in these single combats with the government that it can defend its rights. In Russia you can always find 10 men who are so loyal to their ideas, who take to heart the unhappiness of their country that it's no sacrifice to die on behalf of their cause. Nothing can frighten such people.*

Judge: *You speak of yourself, what was, not of what will be.*

Sasha: *I cannot say.*

Judge: *So, under influence of these thoughts you decided to participate in this evil deed?*

Sasha: *My intention was to show terror as the unavoidable consequence of existing conditions and contradictions of life. We* *can develop our intellectual capacities, but we have little chance of putting them at the service of our country. Her classes are not full-grown. So a revolutionist thinks in terms of bombs, coup d'etats, and violence. Don't you agree?*

Judge: You're on trial, not I. (Aside.) How admirable. He's got the guts of his convictions. (Gaveling.) Defendant is found guilty without remorse.

Mom: *No. Give him to me. I'll purge his heart of criminal thoughts, castrate him, bring back his healthy instincts. Sasha, tell them you're sorry.*

Sasha: *Try to understand. Imagine two men at a pistol duel. One shoots, misses; and as the other takes aim the first one asks him not to shoot. I can't do that. What can one say in a minute, I love you, embrace, kiss, hug one's brothers and sisters? There is only time to die with dignity. I believe in fairness, truth; prefer tact to confrontation. I like using my hands. I built pieces of furniture and gave them away. I learned chess at seven, even beat father once. But mostly I liked truth. Truth and honesty always touched a sympathetic chord in me. I abhorred hypocrisy. When fellow students were arrested for being outspoken, it would've been amoral of me to say nothing; and yet government officials display an aversion to human language, to cries for decency, and respect for individuality.*

Mom: Will you receive God's blessing?

Sasha: I ask forgiveness for my acts and thoughts which belong to you, babushka. Let the world become a better place. Help it live in peace.

Lenin: All of this set me thinking of the futility of lives spent hoping for justice, that truth would always triumph, and leaders would adjust their oppressive behavior. Sash's fate brought my first glimpse of rebellion, and the conscious thought that only a radical approach plus the will to succeed could overcome the monarchy. So, I decided on a different path.

Sasha: I consider intelligence and education to be a gift—

Lenin: It was not necessary to be a bomb thrower oneself.

Sasha: Not a right to abuse others less endowed. I am not given to mischief and dramatics or obsessions of revenge. I believe in truth, kindness and consideration of people. At the university I began seriously working in zoology. I had in mind to—well; I always loved natural history, philosophy, and languages. Right, Little Barrel? (Lenin joins Sasha on walk to the gallows.) The times we spent in my room.

Lenin-Sasha: Bursting with life! Butterfly nets, test tubes. Leaves pressed between pages, jars with specimen from the Sviaga River. Remember? We'd swim and fish in the meandering Sviaga. I remember you were impertinent and talked back to Mom.

Lenin: I never—

Sasha: Never when Dad was around.

Lenin: Remember what we'd say when boring people came calling, especially dull relatives? We'd say—

Lenin-Sasha: Oblige us with your absence! Ha, ha, ha!

Sasha: Once you nearly drowned in the river.

Lenin: A ditch full of water by the river. Someone said there was a carp in it. I looked and looked and fell in. The mud at the bottom sucked me down. Someone walking by, a factory worker, saved me.

Sasha: There'll be no such fellow coming by for me. Oh, but if all we had was our childhood together—what's so bad? Ice skating on Sviaga, the sharp steep slopes no one would try but us. Flying like no one else Flying like no one dared even on a sled! Down and up and round and down, down into the smooth skating rink. Oh, I was a good skater. Oh, what guts we had. Nothing timid about the Ulyanov brothers. (Pause.) Goodbye, Volodya, Little Barrel. Keep your pencil sharp as a stiletto.

(Drum roll; gallows in silhouette; Sasha goes toward it; Lenin follows.)

Lenin-Sasha: Oblige us with your absence! Ha, ha! (Lines split between them.) Remember Kouskino . . . the white house with columns . . . steamer up the Volga to Kazan . . . the carriage ride to the summer house everyone crammed in tight among wicker hampers. Whole summers, no work. All play. The days merged one into the other. Where did it go, all those summers? They seem like one endless day. Look, Sash, my pencil: sharp as a stiletto. Race you to the river Ushna. Last one in is a bore!

Lenin: Heine's ok, but Turgeniev: "Country gentlemen in our youthful boredom like a mushroom frying in sour cream."

Sasha: (Breaks off, runs, arms open, leaps into the audience, screaming.) They rob us of our youth, kill our finest impulses, steal our dreams!
Lenin: *Sasha!*
(Sound Effect: resounding slam of gallows trap door; Lenin's shout melts into shrieking train whistle, horses whinnying, galloping hooves.)

Scene 3:
Chess On Capri:
The Romance of Freedom

Time: July 1908, late morning.
Place: Villa Blaesus o Settianni, south side of Capri, Italy.
Characters: Coachie; Mamushka; Lenin, 38; Bogdanov; 30's; Lunacharsky, 30's; Maximovitch Gorky, 40's, his wife Marya, 30's; two young servants.

Coachie: This is Villa Blaesus o Settianni on Capri, a small, mountainous Mediterranean island off the bay of Naples with magnificent, breath taking panoramic views of sea and sky.
Mamushka: Ok. It's not the steppes.
Coachie: Capri is famous for curative powers—
Mamushka: So is Siberia. Tfu!
Coachie: The dry air and mountain climate is conducive to building the lungs, cleansing the bronchial tubes—
Mamushka: And your pocket.
Coachie: The azure blue sky, the translucent ocean, the sweet smell of orange blossoms are a far cry from the bathetic, musty, gray gloom of cities full of the wild and dreamy-eyed living syphilitic lives of compromise, degradation, and false assumptions who end up dying of slow disappointment. The villa is accessible by funicular.
Mamushka: Fun-what?
Coachie: A railway worked by a rope. You pull yourself up.

Mamushka: It's not for everybody. (Pokes his belly.)
Coachie: Villa Blaesus sits on a cliff above a sheltered cove, the Marina Piccola, and the stupendous Augustus Gardens. Here, the only call is the sun, sea, n' the plaintive shepherd's flute. From the veranda the ocean spreads before us under the southern sun as yachts toss and dip. Here one feels weightless, intoxicated by a translucent sea, expansive sky, n' soft sea breezes, drifting in bowers of sweet smelling orange blossoms, frangipani, myrtle—
Mamushka: I feel like I'm being embalmed alive.
Coachie: And pine trees lazily dropping pinecones,—Tfu! Tfu! Tfu!—Which are beaten on rock for the savory pinole nut within. Famous people come here: aristocrats, artists, Bohemians, n' homosexuals.
Mamushka: So on Capri the pinole is not the only nut.
Coachie: Presently, Maximovitch Gorky occupies the villa, and has three houseguests.
Mamushka: A houseguest is like fish, after three days it stinks.
Coachie: Three Bolsheviks.
Mamushka: Make that three minutes.
Coachie: All high-ranking and disputatious Party officials at odds over Party Doctrine. By inviting them on holiday Gorky hopes that on tranquil Capri calmer minds will heal the breech.
Mamushka: Tfu! Good luck to him. Three Bull-sheviks can only make a decision if two are absent.
(Lights up on villa veranda finds Lenin self-absorbed; Lunacharsky and Bogdanov playing chess.)
Mamushka: Listen, quit shilly-shallying. Get on with the squalid truth as it happened, not as it appears to the imagination of someone covering his tracks,—Tfu!—Or, to *writers* n' *intellectuals* who romanticize revolutions as glorious attempts to better mankind. Tfu! In the end *all revolutions eat their children. Better to let people be.* (THEY fade into BG.)
(Enter Marya, servants with breakfast placed on a side table; exit servants.)
Marya: Bu-on gior-no. (All rise courteously but Lenin.) Colazione. Help yourselves: tea, café, biscotti. (Cranks phonograph; dances to a waltz.)
Lunacharsky: Colazione. That's a word you can eat. Colazione!

Bogdanov: Croissant bumps biscotti, Comrade Colazione.
(Gradually, the players move in rhythm. Lunacharsky picks up a piece, waltzes around the table, returns, and places it.)
Lunacharsky: Knight takes castle.
Bogdanov: (Does same going opposite way.) Queen takes knight.
(While playing Lunacharsky dances with Marya; Bogdanov with a chair.)
Marya: It's the music of the stars.
Lunacharsky: Now where was I?
Bogdanov: Fashioning a colazione.
Lunacharsky: Antipasto, primo piato, secondo piato, mangia questo! Ha!
(Several fast moves are slammed down hard.)
Bogdanov: How is it with you this morning, Marya?
Marya: Waltzing along, waltzing along amidst the usual gang of exiles and émigrés coming, going, drinking, arguing, and always requesting money for hotel bills. You'd think Max was the Bank of England.
Lunacharsky: I wonder, does it rain much up here? What's thunder like in the clouds? Mightier than a king's crown, I should think.
(Each man moves a piece.)
Marya: Sometimes. Other times it's a feint, distant tambourine bringing rain tinkling like an ankle bracelet.
Bogdanov: Now I know where Max gets his poetry. Let's hear more.
Marya: More you shall have. With Max I rarely get a word in edgewise. You know what men's jewelry is? A chest full of medals. But forget that. Rather let us think of the gentle rain that comes early in the morning like rabbit feet rustling on the roof, and often enough to keep Capri plush.
Lunacharsky: The view is delicious, Marya. (Lowered voice.) Good for a taste, but as a steady diet, too complacent.
Bogdanov: Even in heaven you would find fault. Ici, malcontento. Bishop takes castle. Delicious, yes?
Lunacharsky: Delicious, no. (Moves piece.) Marya, is it proper to say Piato primo e piato secondo? Are "o" endings correct?

Marya: The "o's" are in place, yes.
Lunacharsky: My "o's" are in place, Bogdanov.
Bogdanov: I'm so glad. Now this move, comrade, should give rise to some "o's", oohs, and ahs. (Takes piece.)
Lunacharsky: The devil take you! It's the altitude. (Moves piece.) My game's off so high up. I feel light headed.
Bogdanov: There isn't enough oxygen in the world to improve your game.
Lunacharsky: True. Still I'm insulted. (Moves a piece with a slam.) I think I'll become a chef. What? I'm serious. In a kitchen you know where you stand. You can get your hands on things. Ingredients c'est tout. You get what you give.
Bogdanov: At the next International wear an apron and chef's hat. (Takes a piece.) Your main dish is lip service. The ingredients are at hand, but not the recipe, unless it's for minestrone. You touched it.
Lunacharsky: No. The hand hovers, that's all. You'd like me to move there, but no. Ici! (Slams down piece. Cautious moves ensue.) A good chef mixes ingredients by intuition, his fingers. Life and chess require understanding ingredients. *What you put in you get out.* But you must also feel how far to go with this or that, how long to cook a dish, and at what temperature. Cooking is autocratic. One chef, one menu. Too many chefs spoil the broth. Next thing the spoon's telling the dish.
Bogdanov: Or the bishop tells the king, checkmate. You trying to sell Ilych's medicine? People are not cabbages. (Leans back.)
Lunacharsky: Marya, this is idyllic: flora, fauna, Fresh air, ocean and sky. What's wrong with this picture?
Bogdanov: You're in it.
Lunacharsky: In no time it will turn you into a potted palm on a veranda to oblivion contented drinking sunshine and completely lost to city life.
Bogdanov: That's a plus not a loss.
Lunacharsky: Then one day the post delivers a draft notice to fight a capitalist war in a foreign land, and all you know is the sun and the Shepard's flute.
Marya: Good morning, Ilych. Café, tea?
Lenin: Yes.

Marya: To which?
Lenin: Which what?
Marya: O, you are lost in the stars. Did you rest well overnight?
Lenin: O, yes. Well, fair. My head ached most of the time. And you?
Marya: I slept the sleep of the dead. Even Maxim's tossing and turning didn't wake me. Next thing it was morning and Max had gone off to class.
Lenin: How is he progressing?
Marya: There are no cures for the incorrigible. In front of me he's good. Behind my back—Well, he's better. How is it with Nadya?
Lenin: Her thyroid's acting up.
Marya: The air here might've helped.
Lenin: Yes. But not the coming and going.
Marya: On the bright side absence makes the heart grow fonder.
Lenin: Have you read the American Whitman? He's Thoreau with wings . . . pines for the evanescent moment: the turning seasons, the leaf that blooms, withers, and dies. I don't usually give into romantic notions. They can be dangerous like music and lead one into complacency and sentimentality in a world that can destroy you in seconds. I should like to sit down with Plato and Shakespeare, and this fellow Walt Whitman. They all have one thing in common. Underneath they're communists. So, too, the early Greeks in their notion of the commune, or Polis, a community based on kinship.
Marya: Sort of an extended family.
Lenin: Yes. And not without family quarrels like what we're going through. All the more bitter because they are family quarrels.
Bogdanov: Ilych, how about a round? You can't win them all.
Lenin: That's my fear.
Bogdanov: Take the black. I won't have to switch seats.
Lenin: I'd like to play the Bard, Plato, and Whitman more to hear their thoughts on everything and nothing. Frankly, there is no difference between poets and politicians. We're all selling dreams.
Marya: Except poets are in earnest and point the way between reality and the soul.
Bogdanov: What way do politicians point?

Lunacharsky: To their next meal ticket. Marya, you're radiant. Max should be wary of flirts.
Marya: Thank you. He's one himself and a gypsy. In fact, you're all gypsies—
Lenin: Not by choice.
Marya: Without country and home.
Bogdanov: Disputatious. Quick to brawl.
Lunacharsky: Chess players and kibitzers with tongues like knives.
Bogdanov: *Ilych,* pick your color and prepare to die. (Commotion off.)
Gorky: (Entering.) Buon giorno a tutti. A comrade in need.
Marya: One of many, you mean. Honestly, Max. You're not the benefactor of every Russian exile. One day the well will dry up.
Lunacharsky: Then call Ilych and he'll expropriate some rubles. (All: Oooh!)
Lenin: Whatever serves the Party.
Marya: For the moment the Party is being served colazione, which is getting colder by the minute. Café, tea, biscotti?
Gorky: Biscotti are for dogs. O, God! My epitaph: *Here lies Gorky, cured of TB, died of starvation. His loving, overbearing wife, Marya.*
Marya: Mine will be briefer: *A wife drained of patience.* Café anyone?
Gorky: (Claps hands.) Allesandra, Giovanni, venite! Two of my students who work here to offset tuition. (They enter.) Ciao. Per piacere. Un piccolo sciocchezza in the spirit of the Comedia dell'Arte?
Giovanni—Allesandra: Benvenuti tuti; amici, nemici. E quazi niente. Applauso. Grazie. Ferme! Applauso. Ferme! (Moving angularly.)
Columbina: I can't marry. You're left, I'm right.
Arlechino: Except back-to-back. Then my left is your right.
Columbina: Don't mix me up.
Arlechino: I love what you stand for even when you're sitting.
Columbina: I'm Marxist to the corpse.
Arlechino: You mean core.
Columbina: No. He's dead. Better be. They buried him.

Arlechino: You love the Party more than Peppino? Can the Party warm your feet at night? Only Peppino can. Peppino pidocchio del Materassa.
Columbina: Actually, I'm a sexual vegetarian. No meat, Tony.
Arlechino: I'm Peppino. What about family, children?
Columbina: Bearers on proxy farms and a crèche. Children will be brought up not knowing their real parents who in turn don't know them. Children will be fed by mothers with full breasts and wet nurses. Comes the revolution work will be ancient history. All we'll do is eat, drink, and make out reports.
Arlechino: If life's perfect what's to report?
Columbina: The Bolsheviks'll think of something. You can't run a country without reports?
Arlechino: I've got a secret. Bolsheviks don't wear underwear.
Columbina: How do you know?
Arlechino: (Fay.) O, jusssst a wild guessss.
Columbina: Goodbye family n' friends. Big deal. Y'can count 'em on one hand anyway. So get aboard the train to Ethiopia.
Arlechino: Y'mean, Utopia.
Columbina: No. Ethiopia. Easier to get to. Go to Morocco and turn left.
Arlechino: A roll in the hay beats an ideal anytime. Let's make love.
Columbina: Love? What's that? Oh! Party protocol forbids fraternization of any kind. It's quite clear, comrade. Page 11; paragraph 5.9, B: "No Sex. We are the Party of no party. (Plays waltz on phonograph.) Besides, I have a personal problem. Trotsky got me pregnant.
Arlechino: Impossible. He's never been to Italy.
Columbina: I meant Stalin.
Arlechino: He's in Tiflis robbing banks.
Columbina: Then it was Lenin.
Arlechino: He just got here.
Columbina: O, I don't know. All those Russians have funny mustaches.
(Servants bow and exit to applause.)
Bogdanov: Maxim, you put them up to that.
Gorky: No, no. The Comedia Del'Arte takes what's in the air.

Lunacharsky: Something's in the air all right.
Lenin: (Sitting.) Monsieur Bogdanov, après vous.
Bogdanov: No. Après vous, s'il vous plait.
Lenin: Aux contraire. If I move first it'll be over that much faster. (Bogdanov moves, Lenin counters, and soon:) Checkmate.
Bogdanov: Damn!
Gorky: Don't nail me to the cross for expediting this talk, but—
Lenin: One can know the game but playing it is another matter. Anticipation and focus c'est tout.
Bogdanov: Ilych, you're dogmatic about everything.
Lunacharsky: Ease up. Let in some light.
Lenin: And one morning you wake up dead.
Marya: May I interject a brief thought? Max and I used to argue a lot. One day a friend said, you argue to hear yourself because in reality you're saying the same thing. Oddly enough we agreed, but kept arguing anyway. The day we started listening to each other the arguing ended.
Gorky: Subsided.
Lenin: I know what is necessary.
Fast Overlapping Voices: And we don't? I didn't say that. It's implied. You're bullheaded. Equivocation is death. Conciliation, my friend. What good is winning the battle if you lose the war? Compromise.
Lenin: Our party can't afford mistakes. The people must fight to recover what was bred out of them, the meaning of the commune, of sharing, of standing up for their rights, of putting the good of the group before the individual. It's been replaced by a sado-masochist pecking order.
Bogdanov-Lunacharsky: O, that's good. Explain it to the peanut gallery.
Lenin: It's an inevitable offshoot of capitalism, and appropriate at this stage of social development. Citizens give up something to get something. Everyone profits at everyone else's expense and those at the bottom get crushed, which is the sacrifice for the good of all. Everyone cowers before those above allowing themselves to be inflicted with pain while in turn sticking it to someone below. Very homogeneous, yes? Everyone submits, relinquishes his rights to the next man up the ladder. Freedom

applies in so far as it advances the good of the group anything less is intolerable. Everyone is ruled along certain proscribed lines. Later, actual philosophy might enter the picture. It's the age-old, how to make an omelet without breaking an egg?
Bogdanov: The question is how many eggs?
Lenin: Governing and revolutions are mysterious things. Nothing is carved in stone.
Bogdanov: The question is how far to go to establish our unproven position.
Lenin: New enterprises require bold initiatives.
Lunacharsky-Bogdanov: How bold? Armageddon?
Gorky: What counts are good intentions and truth.
Lenin: Rome wasn't built in a day, or with love and kisses.
Bogdanov-Lunacharsky: But there was a foundation. All we have is pie-in-the-sky theory.
Lenin: Our doctrine will see us through. No deviation from the plan.
Bogdanov: Leadership ought to be by example of free speech in an open public forum that considers all sides and opinions . . . a duma composed of representatives from around the country.
Lenin: Industrialized Germany is ready for it, but Russia will take time, and patience. Change is rarely as simple as it appears in theory. There will be resistance that must be dealt with firmly.
Bogdanov: Meaning?
Lenin: Strong leadership will be necessary to get the system moving.
Lunacharsky: An individual, or group?
Lenin: At first perhaps a strong leader resting on an inner circle of advisors, or cadre. Politics and leadership are not stagnant, but constantly evolving and require flexible leadership.
Gorky: That would take a great amount of trust in someone, or some group. But who?
Lunacharsky: I prefer leadership by consensus.
Bogdanov: A parliamentary approach.
Lenin: In the end, yes, but on the way quick decisions may be necessary, which if put to a vote can lose the advantage of timeliness. Consensus is the end goal once the game is underway

and a "doctrine" established. Life is constantly evolving. It takes flexible thinking, fearless thinking, and taking gutsy chances.

Lunacharshky: A gospel according to Lenin.

Lenin: No plan is fool proof. It merely allows for a foothold in a crisis, and helps to avoid extreme errors, or looking foolish standing around wondering what next. The plan includes contingencies, and eliminates navigating in the dark. Later, parliamentary methods can be introduced. Napoleon was right.

All: On s'engage et puis on voit, engage and then see.

Gorky: Who do you trust in the kitchen? That's the question.

Lunacharsky: Mamushka, who else? (All: Ha, ha.)

Lenin: Writing and engaging in politics is mixing apples and oranges. Max, you have great compassion and understanding of human behavior. But you fall short in grasping the conflict between classes and subtleties of class relations. You took my part, I admit, in your paper with your article 'Don't Touch Lenin' more as a friend of Vladimir Ulyanov, someone you respect, rather than as Lenin, spokesman and defender of the people. Politics engages in real human relationships, whereas, writing is wishful thinking.

Gorky: Granted. But a strange thing happens in good writing. In the end the whole is organic. After pushing and shoving A follows B and there is no other possibility.

Lenin: Writing is representational, living is presentational, unpredictable, fluid and visceral with hot blood coursing in its veins. If I meddled in your work doubtless you'd say, what the devil does Lenin know about poetry, character development, and plot? It is impermissible for a politician to dwell in some idyllic glade apart from his constituency. Poets dream, politicians live. It's the living that's toughest, yes, prosaic, often vulgar, and one's life is forfeit at a moment's notice. You luxuriate in hindsight, but if I forget the people my goose is cooked. Bogdanov's article *Politics and Philosophy* was irresponsible.

Bogdanov: Well, you came to that through the back door.

Gorky: When chickens finish quarreling over food they often find there is plenty to go around.

Lenin: Advising others is like handing a mirror to the blind.

Lunacharsky: Sticking our heads in the sand will only make matters worse. There is more than one way to skin a cat.
Lenin: We're not speaking of cats, but people. Hardnosed Marxian materialism in theory must be applied practically. You would mix philosophy and politics with compromise. Soon you'd be back on the street.
Lunacharsky: And you would shoot everyone who disagrees, who says this is the path of least resistance, of less bloodshed.
Gorky: There is truth on both sides. Sometimes bending is necessary.
Lunacharsky: It boils down to who controls the party.
Gorky: Soon there won't be a Party.
Lenin: It takes a firm hand and willingness to do whatever it takes.
Bogdanov: "Whatever it takes" is a broad statement.
Gorky: This haggling has caused discord, disaffection, dissention, and weakened the Party ranks.
Lenin: Let no one think that the world can be ruled without blood.
Bogdanov: Martov is right.
Lenin: It runs on intolerance and political decadence. We must go slowly.
Gorky: For my part I am not entirely opposed to Martov.
Lunacharsky: A brilliant theorist and orator.
Bogdanov: Breaking with Martov is wrong. We must go slowly.
Lenin: We're not playing turtle and hare. Martov's erudition is hollow and lacks action.
Bogdanov: He raises the question—
Lenin: But never the solution. He's a bourgeois conciliator who suffers from that fatal Menshevik disease indecisiveness. He lacks the esdential revolutionary will-power. As usual he gives a brilliant speech, but fails to say what to do. No words of action, which are desparately needed.
Bogdanov-Lunacharsky: Not everyone moves in your tempo, Ilych. Or your *indelicate* style. We do not condone bank robbery to support the Party. Calling it "expropriation" merely eases your conscience.
Lenin: The wish does not become the act sticking to principles.

Bogdanov: It's unscrupulous behavior.
Lenin: There is no sanitary solution to freedom. The moment you stand on principles your opponent shifts position and knifes you in the back. Socialism can't be implemented by kind thoughts and indecisive acts.
Gorky: Every soul is conflicted. No one is content. Business reflects it.
Lunacharsky-Bogdanov: The French Revolution had a noble purpose. But got lost.
Lenin: The only way out is to go through. History shows that success in Revolutions is generally proportionate to their power of adaptation and re-absorption of what they rebelled against. Societies do not run on good intentions. Democracy has evils, corruptions, incompetence, and its own subtle tyranny based on capitalism. The good is not liberty, but wisdom and contentment with one's natural restrictions. Let's be grateful to democracy for opening the great free-for-all, catch-as-catch can wrestling match of laissez-faire industrialism.
Lunacharsky: This is your grand polemic to justify thievery.
Lenin: You want polite words and encomiums while the noose is slipped round your neck. Bah! A thousand reforms have left the world as corrupt as ever. Each reform has founded a new institution, which has bred its own congenial abuses. What form of society is best? None. There's not much difference among them. Plato suggests timocracy, a government based solely on merit and honor.
Gorky-Lunacharsky: That's even beyond Utopia. Aristocracy all over again.
Lenin: But not hereditary. Everyone would have a clear path to rise up according to ability—incompetence would be a disqualifier no matter how rich or important or furnished with plebiscites. A government based on equality of opportunity would be a synthesis of democracy-aristocracy ruled by Plato's philosopher kings. The cause of war has always been property. All property has its origin in violence and theft. The Kimberly diamond mines, the Rand gold mines of Africa are merely transitions of robbery into property. No good to the community comes from private ownership of land. If men were reasonable—but they are not.—They would decree an

end to ownership with a moderate lifetime compensation to the present owners.

Gorky: Such a tall order, comrade.

Lenin: Private property is protected by the state and robberies that make property are sanctioned by legislation and enforced by arms and war. The state is a great evil and should be taken over by cooperatives and producer syndicates.

Bogdanov: What about personality, individuality?

Lenin: Crushed by the state into rote conformity. Only the greater safety and orderliness of modern life can reconcile us to the state. Our struggle is the *romance of truth.*

Gorky: Here, here. Well put. Openness and freedom enables personality. There is no freedom in communism only subordination, which brings us back to square one.

Lenin: Communism is freedom without self-indulgence.

Gorky: Pure semantics. All roads lead to Rome. It's supreme egotism to bust up a chance to get there because your road is the best way.

Lunacharsky-Bogdanov: Here! Here!

Lenin: You want to fight the gentleman's battle. Hooray for you, says your opponent, laughing up his sleeve because he has no intention of playing fair, but like all sly thieves will be quick to be indignant when bested. They hold allegiance principles like you in theory but disregard them in practice. Come. You know it. We dared to speak out, had the audacity to demand accountability, and the government's answer was not objective consideration of legitimate demand, but a sentence of life in exile. Our lives attest to the deceitful power of the state right or wrong. How can either of you look in the mirror and say otherwise?

Bogdanov: Because I am not corrupted.

Lunacharsky: Exactly. We have not stooped to their level of vulgarity.

Lenin: Congratulations. Meanwhile, enjoy the view knowing you will never go home again; never see your loved ones ever again because you cling to your spotless integrity, which others use for a doormat. More is the pity. Wake up, comrades. (Pounds fist.) Take the bit between your teeth, but don't get squeamish with each jerk of the reins. Be resolute, resolute! Life or death! No in between. Like our brothers and sisters before us, we must mount the barricades, put our bodies on the line, flesh against steel, and stand firm no matter what. Principles and ethics are mere words in a children's fairy tale. I'm right, you're right. We're all right. It is they who are in the wrong. What got us exiled was wishing and dreaming, acting by impractical standards. Do you want to win or settle for second best and feeling good about it because you acted correctly, stuck to your fine principles, played fair and square with robbers and thieves? No. I will fight tooth and nail to gain a foothold. In me, they shall meet their match, a worthy adversary, no mealy mouth, and dreamy-eyed innocent afraid of getting mud on his face. This is no game of Troika, comrades. We are not Don Quixote tilting at windmills, Mr. Nice Guy thrilled to be in the game and as always grateful to be holding the short end of the stick. Bah! Tfu!

Bogdanov-Lunacharsky: Cruel only to be kind. Is that it? Freedom is the supreme good. Freedom of thought and action. Only through free discussion can we pick our way through the rubble of errors and prejudices to the truth. Hatred and war come largely from fixed ideas or dogmatic faith. Were we to sink to their level where is the guarantee we'd be any better than those we deposed?

Lenin: Because you act for the good of others and have never lied to yourself.

Lunacharsky-Bogdanov: Say you? Faith and trust? E tu, Brute. Some things readily become habit forming.

Lenin: Not if you have never relinquished who you are and your ultimate purpose. The weak shall succumb as always. It's to be expected. Unlikely heroes are forged in battle. Stay true to yourself and you win the day. This I believe but only if you are strong willed and not just children playing with wooden swords. Strategy and plans are fine but in the heat of battle opportunity and fortune win the day.

Lunacharsky: Death wins the day.

Gorky: Cowards die a thousand deaths, heroes die once.

Lenin: One of our first steps should we gain power is implementation of universal schooling to root out the old thinking. Education should be the development of a scientific habit of mind. The goal is to rid us of the impulses and desires that center round possessions. There is nothing man might not do if our organizations of schools and universities were properly developed, manned, and directed intelligently to reconstruction of human character. This, not violent revolution, or paper legislation, is the way out of economic greed and international brutality. Schools are the open sesame to Utopia.

Gorky: Here, here.

Bogdanov: Even the Mensheviks disapprove of expropriation.

Lenin: Get your priorities straight. What we *expropriate* is "stolen goods". The government steals from the people and we steal it back. They make promises, don't deliver, and the people's money ends up in the pockets of corrupt ministers and their cronies. We use it to educate the people and to keep the cause of the people alive. You make a living writing. They pay you to feed their souls. What we take goes to feed their minds and bellies, to break them from that lethargy of blind devotion to an oligarchy that spits in their face. Don't be so quick to condemn us. What we take means that much less goes to support a rotten system. They bleed the people, we bleed them, and our efforts re-infuse the people with hope. Government is the thief, not us. They lost creditability long ago. The wonder is why the people tolerate obvious abuse. They're bound to rebel sooner or later and then there will be hell to pay. The reality of government hinges on people who at bottom can't be trusted. The question is not government but people—

Gorky: A work in progress.

Lenin: Government officials force issues, get presumptuous, pass laws that try to remake human beings and refashion society often without a mandate and against the people's will. Change takes blood and sweat.

Bogdanov: How much?

Lenin: Whatever it takes.

Lunacharsky: Your argument has contradictions. Freedom on one hand and control on the other. Vinegar and oil.

Bogdanov: You would legislate freedom.

Lenin: At first, yes. Laws would be needed to turn the ship around.

Gorky: Then what?

Lenin: When people begin to think justly there is no need of laws.
Gorky: At bottom you're an artist. You think you can reshape people like a sculptor molding clay. Many tried and failed. The job is beyond any one man or group. No. I'm wrong. It's worked in part in democratic America. They accept a certain amount of larceny as a given and jail those who go too far. That is, the ones who get caught. The sin in America as in Greek times, is not the criminal act, but getting caught. People are jailed for getting caught not for committing crimes.
Lenin: You weave a nice story. One can't contradict or disprove opinion. You may be right. Legislation does not change human nature. Change must be cultivated, pushed along like a baby in a stroller. Time is the mother, time and rethinking. Change starts in school and it won't be overnight but over several generations. I would like the Mensheviks to be part of our drive toward that end, but I can't accept their idea of cooperating with the Duma. No conciliation with those bourgeois phoney flunkies of the monarchy who smile and kill you at the same time. And the Cadets? Bah! Worms in the grave of revolution. I believe in organized and armed insurrection. We're not playing at Troika. See the pretty soldiers marching off to war, the band playing. So thrilling. When I grow up I want to wear a uniform, go to war, fight, and come marching home a hero with the band playing, people cheering. Wonderful! But what of the dead, maimed, and crippled? O, in my war nobody dies and everyone wins. Wonderful! But in real war people die. They do? Yes. For keeps? Yes. And they never see their mothers again? O, I don't like this game. I'm not playing anymore. I'm going home to mamushka. Childish? Yes. But mothers know instinctively right from wrong. So did we once. What changed?
Gorky: Growing up is serious business.
Bogdanov: Murderous.
Gorky: It doesn't have to be.
Lenin: We were doing fine until you came in.
Gorky: Harmless games never solve anything. Sorry. Maybe I should rent another villa.

Lunacharsky-Bogdanov: Whatever serves the Party. Just pay the bills. If you're funds are low Ilych will expropriate some. "Whatever serves the Party" is a dangerous notion.
Lenin: I should've been a mountain shepherd tending sheep and goats. Instead I find pigs at the trough.
Lunacharsky: You go too far. We are not pigs or sheep except in your presumptuous mind. Frankly, you already have the makings of a good dog to enforce your position in that crass and bizarre Djugasvilli, or Ioseph, or Stalin, or whatever he calls himself.
Bogdanov: Ah, yes. The Tiflis expropriator.
Lunacharsky: A word to the wise.
Lenin: Every man has his value.
Lunacharsky: Keep that one on a short leash. Now then. I shall destroy you inside of 15 moves.
Lenin: Why so long? I concede the first move to my opponent.
Lunacharsky: I give it to you. Red or white, your choice? Take the red and I won't have to change seats. Wait. How foolish of me. We'll turn the board around.
Lenin: The fault dear Brutus, is not in who has what color, but that in chess you are all underling, as Gorky can attest to after many defeats—(All: Boo! Here! Here!) It's really a question of how many moves will it take before you go down. Eight moves. I feel merciful.
Lunacharsky: Taking control already. Chew on this.
All: One.
Lenin: (Counters.) No. Count my moves only.
(Lunacharsky rasies hand, circles it, moves piece; Lenin counters.)
All: Two! (Lunacharsky counters; Lenin counters.) Three!
Lenin: I already see an early demise. Don't think. I'll always be two steps ahead. (Lenin yawns; Lunacharsky moves, Lenin counters.)
All: Four! (Lunacharsky thinks, moves; Lenin counters.) Five!
Lenin: I wonder was it safe up here when Vesuvius erupted, the air full of ghostly soot? Probably like sticking your head down a chimney with a fire blazing in the hearth while the roof is caving in.
Lunacharsky: An apt description of playing chess with you. (Lunacharsky moves then changes his mind.)

Lenin: Too late. You let go. Checkmate.
All: Bravo! In six. Ilych, you're a wonder!
Gorky: Now, gentlemen, what do you say to cards on the table?
Lenin: No good can come mixing philosophy with politics. We must be pragmatic not abstract.
Bogdanov: We believe in conciliation.
Lunacharsky: It's good common sense to leave our options open.
Lenin: We must stand firm and united.
Bogdanov: Agreed.
Lenin: Those in power will not quit because we wish it so.
Lunacharsky: True.
Lenin: Carpe diem quam minimus credula postero—enjoy today, trust little to tomorrow. When our time comes, we must seize it by any means. But make no mistake. There is bound to be bloodshed. Let it be on their hands, which are already bloodied enough.
Gorky: (Takes a biscotti, puts it back.) Carpe diem, seize the day.
Lenin: Argument is part and parcel of the growth process, the aches and pains of finding common ground. I can't see the value of mixing politics and philosophy when heads are being cracked and necks broken.
Lunacharsky: The Paris Commune ended in death and Napoleon.
Lenin: The tactics of those in power have always been dirty. Yet knowing this you want to play nice. Look where nice put us. You've a list of do's and don'ts. I have no such list. I know the reality of our situation. You're still playing childish games of wishing and hoping and compromising. It's utter rubbish to think you can strike bargains with liars and double dealers. If history has taught us anything it's that the nobility, the ruling classes broke faith with people a thousand years ago. The nobility will never have a change of heart because, thanks to the people's acquiescence, its heels are dug in too deep. They like the luxury of their life-style too much to give it up. In fact, it's our fault that they see themselves to the manner born and have come to believe see themselves as demi Gods, and the rest of us filth and chattel. No, sir. I make no conciliation with dishonorable people.

They must be destroyed lock, stock, and barrel. The evidence is abundantly clear. I say, annihilate them! Grind them into the dust to avoid a second coming.
Lunacharsky—Bogdanov: God! Such bitterness, Ilych. Where does it come from? Where's your compassion?
Lenin: History favors the bold, my friend. I am fed up to the gills with self-serving, failed leadership, and a track record long and bloody.
Gorky: For my part I'll take mama in the kitchen singing folk songs while pies and breads bake in the oven.
Lenin: You can afford that sort of thinking writing in your ivory tower, but reality is different. Government is by the book and insensitive, a book containing the lives of the people forfeited in defense of capitalist, carte blanche usury. You find levity in that, eh? I don't. Write all the books you want, earn the respect and love of the people with your poetry, but get in the way of government and you're a dead duck.
Bogdanov: Ilych, criminal acts make us no better than them.
Lenin: True, but that's half the equation. We do not act for personal aggrandizement, but to better the lot of the people. Even the most backward farmer knows, you can't make an omelet without breaking an egg.
Bogdanov: How many eggs, Ilych, are you ready to break?
Lenin: Whatever it takes: hell, fire—
Bogdanov: Armageddon.
Lenin: Out of the ashes a new phoenix shall rise. A dictatorship of the proletariat.
Bogdanov: Spilling blood doesn't bother you?
Lenin: History proves that in revolutions there are no half measures. Monarchists, capitalists, imperialists, whatever their brand, they have killed, and continue to kill millions of people in the name of their cause. Well, I say, if it must be, let the world burn for justice. The nobility and the masses, each entrenched by habit in the old ways, brainwashed for centuries!—They won't change because we wish it so. Words are smoke rings not leadership. Politics is visceral engagement with *consequences*. I accept the challenge.
Bogdanov: We all do.

Lenin: No. You want the results, but fear the consequences. My brother died for Russia. It will not be in vain.
Gorky: Such a travesty. Clearly, there is more that unites you than not.
Lenin: We are all in the same boat only some oars are pulling in the wrong direction. The Tsar of himself is nothing. The danger is his hired guns, the police and Cossacks. Well, we'll hire our own guns. Leading is not for the feint hearted. Mistakes cost blood. If we wish to succeed we must be of a single mind, merciless, and relentless. But proper organization can avoid excesses and bloodshed. We must create fighting units, use insurgency tactics, and that can't be done without vigilant control.
Lunacharsky-Bogdanov: Expropriations. Hired guns. Where does it end? It can get out of control.
Lenin: There's no crime in stealing stolen money. Capitalists do it everyday on the stock exchange.
Gorky: In New York, City of the Yellow Devil.
Lenin: Money taken from a bank is the people's blood money better served in our hands. An organization needs weapons against opposition. From the barricades we must beat out of the ignorant masses centuries of blind devotion to the Little Father, and instill in them self rule, communal work, sharing, each according to his ability to each according his needs. Kant would agree: man must not be used as a means for the ends of others, but must be regarded as an end in himself.
Lunacharsky-Bogdanov: Your readiness to sacrifice lives is scary. Monstrous! Violations of ethics and common sense. You would ignore the well-being and even the lives of people for the unproven ideal. But those lives are real, whereas the ends are always nebulous and often unattainable.
Gorky: Moral principle well taken. Everyone has the right to sacrifice himself for a cause he deems deserving. No one has the right to sacrifice others, or to incite others to sacrifice themselves for that ideal.
Bogdanov: (Moves chess piece.) We have differing concepts or ideology on how best to approach and implement the same goal. The difference is between the scientific—predictive-analytical-

determinist side of the Marx Doctrine, and its revolutionary-hortatorical-moralistic-practical side.

Lenin: Very descriptive erudition beyond understanding.

Bogdanov: From an analytical point of view, maybe Marx can read the future or at least interpret social events and problems world-wide, even presume to advise foreign leaders what the outcome might be if this and thus happens. But no one can say definitely. Marxism may well be the driving force needed to move people to fight and put their lives on the line for revolution and the world victory of the proletariat.

Lunacharsky-Bogdanov: Or a lot of hooey. A means for someone to take control. A conduit marking the egoistic aims of a handful of power hungry individuals to get the workers to do their bidding.

Lenin: Legitimizing the regime comes first. Correct?

Bogdanov: Yes.

Gorky: All this rigmarole makes me hungry. Ultimately, we're all drummers whistling in the dark. Unfortunately, some people can't carry a tune.

Bogdanov: A dictatorship is not necessarily bad, nor is democracy or socialism necessarily good. It's the character of rulers that counts. Ilych refuses to budge from a position of absolutism. Any deviation from *the* Doctrine is heresy.

Lenin: It's only a road map to keep one oriented in a direction.

Lunacharsky: Let's put out a travel book: Bolshevism, The Road to Eden. Take the funicular to the Villa Blaesus and go right to sleep.

Gorky: Asleep you don't hurt people.

Bogdanov: But even Capri wasn't enough for the ancients.

Gorky: Men prefer the illusive to certainty. We were happiest in mamushka's womb. Look around: a shimmering pastel blue sky divided by a thin line marking the horizon, and beyond is Utopia. Sadly, the more you go to it the more it recedes. Gentlemen, where we are at any moment in time, that's Utopia.

Bogdanov: If so, what's the problem?

Gorky: Presumption, mortality, egotism, and willfulness. What is this penchant for the dirty city? It's a combination of the death wish and herd instinct. We love to move in packs, in the safety

of numbers, and yet we know the herd can turn on a whim, stampede, and trample us to death.
Lunacharsky: Sometimes I think this sharing idea in socialism is really an impossible attainment given the nature of people. Be honest. We're kleptomaniacs. We like to steal. I suspect the hope under socialism is that people will steal a little less. How do we reconcile all the fancy abstract thinking with reality?
Lenin: Talking is true, but reality is not.
Gorky: There is a Russian parable called The Mad Chauffeur. It asks the question, What Would You Do? A young man and his mother are in a troika speeding down a steep and precipitous road driven by a reckless, incompetent chauffeur who was perhaps insane, you could try to take over the reins yourself by force but can it be done on a steep mountain road? However skilful you are, however strong, the reins are actually in his hands. He is after all steering the bloody troika! One mistake on a turn or a hesitation of his hand, and the troika is doomed. You know and he knows it and he ridicules your anxiety, your helplessness. "Dare to touch me, he says. I dare you! So you leave the reins in the hands of this mad chauffeur. Moreover you will not hinder, but advise him, assisting, warning him. It is only right. This is what must be done. But you realize such restraint is of no avail, and even with your help the chauffeur can't handle it. Moreover, your old mother senses danger, begs you to help. Misunderstanding your conduct, she accuses you of indifference and inaction. So, What Would You Do?
Lenin: That is our dilemma. Maxim, you are a renowned writer. I wouldn't think of encroaching on your territory, but leave politics to those who know what drives it. You write. We engage. We are grist for your mill, the prose you turn into poetry. You need us. We need you. Well, not you. Give me Turgeniev.
Gorky: Who's she?
Lenin: Seasons turn, trees live and die, and all of it falls into a landscape painting or snapshot. But humans bring another element to the table, intrigue and a will. In any fight the best you can hope for is to come out unscathed.
Gorky: The real miracle is that we come out at all.

Lenin: You plead for love and restraint. But history tells a different story. Survival takes heat, forge and hammer. My brother's death crystallized a truth in me. I was 17 yet I sensed a peculiar awakening. At first I denied the truth. It was incomprehensible. Sasha hanging from a rope? Who would do that to another human being? It was too hideous to contemplate. Any minute he'd come through the door with that smile on his face. Reality struck with such a shocking force that I held the world accountable. It needed routing out, societies reorganized, new principles established, new priorities set on how to live in a civilized manner. All of this meant upheaval, death, and destruction. I decided to pay the price with my life, my freedom, a family, the death of loved ones. What was clear to me then as now is that *revolution is an idea that possesses bayonets*. France went amok because they lacked organization. Bayonets without organization lead to chaos and Napoleon. The old order will not go willingly. It takes expropriation and bayonets to boot them out.

Gorky: Not all, Ilych. Some have little recourse.

Lenin: Nothing personal here, but writers have the luxury of wishful thinking, whereas real life is not an artist's sitting model. It's fluid.

Gorky: Improvisational.

Lenin: S'engage et puis on voit.

Gorky: Curtain down, mon ami. (Moves a piece.)

Lenin: (Counter checkmate.) C'est tout! In capturing me I capture you. Organization, comrade. Thinking ahead. Very critical. (Resets pieces.)

Gorky: You continue to surprise me.

Lenin: I'm glad I don't bore you. Implementation follows organization.

Gorky: What's that you say?

Lenin: Once revolution is achieved, the next step is building a solid economic apparatus with help from the old capitalist organization.

Gorky: That sounds dangerous.

Lenin: But necessary to aid in an apprentice period to facilitate a smooth transition to the new order. Then, rule from the bottom moves into the driver's seat. One has to be prepared for counter-revolution, and how to keep government running. The French struggled for years.

Marya: Out of which came the grand decision maker, the guillotine.

Lenin: Whatever form the people used to pay back their oppressors they learned from them. Revolution is a question of the immovability of the people, how to harness their power and what to do once it starts moving.

Gorky: Your use of the word harness conjures images of yolks and mouth bits, which have always been the peasant's lot.

Lenin: Peasants reign in farm animals, the monarchy reigns in peasants.

Marya: Farmers don't abuse their animals, unless they're fools.

Lenin: There is great power residing in the people, but their minds are stuck in the ice of the great Russian Winter. They see what is happening but cannot lift themselves out of their frozen torpor. Maximevitch, were you ever incarcerated? (He nods yes.) Jail creates writers. Plenty of time to think with few distractions.

Gorky: Writing is a form of imprisonment. But the thought of not being able to step out into the world for a change in scenery would destroy me.

Lenin: In jail it's sink or swim. Writing keeps you from going mad.

Gorky: It didn't stop Gogol.

Lenin: In jail even dullards become resourceful. They learn to pass messages, tap out a communication code with neighbors, how to use invisible ink, milk and lemon juice, when the paper is passed over a flame the words turn brown. Bread rolled into a spongy ball pressed into a well makes a good inkstand.

Gorky: And the guards?

Lenin: I had a few close calls. When the jailer came around I'd swallow the evidence. One day I swallowed six inkwells.

Gorky: What did you write with?

Lenin: A mattress feather, a sharp fingernail.

Gorky: When first I saw you years ago I never thought that you, the quietest man sitting on the stage, would end up outshining them all.

Lenin: What do you mean by quiet? (Lenin sets pieces, moves; Gorky counters.)
Gorky: Marya, look. I'm in a fix already. (Lenin moves; Gorky pursues.)
Marya: O, good move, Max, on behalf of Ilych.
Lenin: In a moment he will go under.
Gorky: On I sois chi mal I pense. (Moves, slams piece down.)
Lenin: In chess, as in life, one must look ahead by at least three moves.
Marya: In competition don't you have to move within a certain time?
Gorky: Are you my wife or his?
Lenin: You can tell Max is a writer by his chess game, which is based on impulse moves. In chess there is no eraser at the end of a pencil. You commit, live and die on each move. Writing has latitude. You can change your mind. Shall I keep talking or are you going to move?
Marya: He writes better than he plays chess.
Lenin: That's not saying much.
Gorky: Silence. I'm trying to coordinate longitude and latitude.
Lenin: Why? The ship is sinking.
Gorky: You're an over confidant bore. Voila! (Moves piece.) Check.
Lenin: Castle to bishop. Checkmate.
Gorky: What?
Lenin: Chess is a bourgeois game infinitely easier to play than life, but similar. You must carry a lot in your noggin, anticipate, and think ahead, or you go under. Here's my secret. I cheat. By planning ahead I cheat the future. Or rather control possibilities.
Gorky: You're formidable, Ilych. I'll give you that.
Lenin: Competing in chess is good. But I don't care for venerating winners, especially to the detriment of the loser. It's a mistake to grab off the lion's share while the other person who may be better than you in other things falls to ruin. What's fare, uplifting or noble in that? It hardly advances a healthy perspective, or a desire to help the less fortunate. In fact, competition is primitive, idolatry, and demoralizing. Though none of the five fingers are equal they do not oppose each other or condescend, but work

in consonance. The right hand does not attack the left except in extreme cases. Capitalism fosters that unwholesome idea: Do unto thy neighbor before he does unto you!

Lunacharsky: To the victor belong the spoils!

Lenin: I win. You lose! A fine kettle of fish, eh? There are participants in every human endeavor whose concerted effort makes possible the highest achievement of the group effort, and the reward ought come in the form of satisfaction of the overall group good. It does not rise above itself but keeps to a spirit of cooperation. Capitalism, the destroyer of humanity, fosters usury and hangs back in step with the atavistic cave man. The dumb are beaten into submission by rules and regulations, which they learn to circumvent while the more clever ones manipulate the greater picture, the so-called public interest. By contrast, chess is based on defined rules, and pieces in plain sight. The rules are constant, but not so in life. Imagine if it were otherwise with each player having a councilor looking on debating each move, and changing the rules whenever they served them? Well that is our government: a minority of inner circles manipulating a figurehead to support itself at the people's expense.

Lunacharsky: Someone is forever bending the rules.

Bogdanov: There is no end to acts of bureaucratic scatterbrain logic that justifies squeezing the life-blood out of people. Object and your branded a malcontent, a criminal, a traitor, and exiled.

Lenin: That's their modus operandi when they know you're onto their game. The people are not stupid. They spoke up in 1905, and have not forgotten that horrible lesson. They appear to have tucked tail, but their anger is fermenting, and one day the sky will fall again here, Germany, and France. Soon the inherent greed of capitalism will devour itself. The greedy paws of European capitalists brought on the Boxer Rebellion, and almost first in line was—

Bogdanov: The Russian government.

Lenin: Which now swears to its 'unselfishness.' It 'unselfishly' began building a railroad through Manchuria under the protection of Russian troops. To call things by their correct names, one must say that the European governments have already commenced partitioning China, not openly, but secretly, like thieves. They have started to rob China as a corpse is robbed, and when this supposed corpse tried to resist—they threw themselves on China like wild beasts, setting fire to entire villages, drowning people in the Amur River, shooting and bayoneting unarmed inhabitants and their wives and children. And all these Christian acts were accompanied by outcries against the *savage* Chinese who dared lift a hand against *civilized* Europeans. (Mocking.) The Tsarist government said these measures are 'temporary,' taken 'exclusively out of necessity to repel the aggressive activities of the Chinese rebels! They are in no sense evidence of selfish plans . . . Poor imperial Russia, so unselfishly Christian. Yet so unjustly insulted! It unselfishly seized Port Arthur several years ago, and it is unselfishly seizing Manchuria. It unselfishly floods the Chinese provinces bordering on Russia with swarms of its contractors, engineers, and officers whose conduct has aroused the indignation even of the Chinese, known for their obedience. The Chinese worker constructing the railway gets 10 kopecks a day for living costs . . . Such a policy is beneficial to a handful of nobles occupying high civil and military positions . . . What good will come to the working class when government uninterruptedly cuts subsidies to starving peasants—bargaining over every kopeck; which cannot find funds for public education; which, like prospering kulak peasants, squeezes the life juice out of workers in state factories, out of petty employees in post offices, and others? The Tsarist government is threatened with bankruptcy yet it wastes money on conquests, holds our people in slavery, but has the audacity to send them to pacify other peoples who rise up against enslavement. It's a black joke on the people, which they don't seem to get except for periodic revolts too few and far between. Revolutions should be on going. It keeps leadership honest.

Lunacharsky: Honest leadership is an oxymoron.

Lenin: The people must continually and forcefully demand accountability from government, and insist forcefully that government pay attention to the interests of those who do not belong to the robber bands at court. The government is like Vaska the Cat. It eats and listens. You talk and it keeps eating.

Lunacharsky: You're Vaska yourself.

Lenin: Maximovitch, you never finished your first impression of me.
Gorky: Ah, yes. But do you really want to hear it? Then bear with me. You struck me as a man incapable of inspiring people to action. I felt a twinge of compassion that day in Southgate seeing you on the dais seated beside all those demonstrative speakers. The bravura and passion of their opinions, the tortuous polemics seemed absolutely confounding, so intricate in detail with statements, counter statements extending like a musical rhythm that lost its initial meter. It required a genius to follow it all. They ranted on and on shouting, hair-splitting minutia, banging the table over this point and that point most of it hyperbole, and yet people applauded, cheering and booing as if they understood. Meanwhile, Ilych cut a low-key figure listening but taking notes and the contrast just didn't add up. I thought, this will surely be the end of him, rolling a guttural 'r" the way you do. Surely, there is some mistake here. You were simple, ordinary, too casual in manner and then that guttural "rrr"—Well, I thought, I've come this far I might as well suffer the rest.
Lenin: I, too, am suffering. Is there more.
Marya: Yes. We're not students in your theatre class. Get on with it.
Lenin: Less sawing of the air.
Marya: But not saw the air thusly.
Gorky: Are you clowns finished?
Lenin: Speaking for myself, no. If you're gathering wool for another story remember to say Ilych loved ice-skating, playing the piano, inexpensive suits, and good shoes which once worn at the heels are tossed away.
Gorky: There's that hand again. You frequently gesture with your hand especially when speaking in public. That exact move changed everything that first day.
Lenin: Which move? This one?
Marya: That's a good one.
Lenin: How about this one?
Marya: Too Italian.
Gorky: I have a move for both of you but I'm too polite to show it. The "r" in combination with the hand and the simplicity of

your words took over and you had everybody eating out of your palm. It dawned on me that you used the trick of simplicity.

Lenin: Assume nothing, never condescend, know your facts and let the cards fall where they may. If you are lucky and the time is ripe, voila! Your unassuming simplicity becomes the subject of critiques and essays. How did he do it? Simple yet profound.

Gorky: Outside of a minute the whole picture changed. At first it was disconcerting to hear intricate political questions explained in simple terms. What was murky polemic became crystal clear and captivating. How you manage it is still a wonder. You're Socrates reincarnated with a vengeance.

Lenin: As a dramatist you have several climaxes building to a denouement, but revolutions have many denouements and many climaxes often without rhyme or reason and moving like some amorphous gluttonous monster with an unquenchable appetite that devours its own and ultimately itself, and leaves the field wide opened to the first screwball that happens along.

Gorky: Bonapartism is unavoidable.

Lenin: But not inevitable.

Lunacharsky: Too many cooks spoil the broth.

Lenin: The adhesive is in the Party Doctrine, the bible, and any deviation whatsoever amounts to heresy.

Bogdanov: Let's be blunt about it. You're looking to be the Pope of the Party.

Lenin: Some voices are stronger than others. In the initial stages a leader with a cadre and then a council. When I was a student in Kazan two ideas stuck in my head, class and class struggle, and the dictatorship of the proletariat. What is class war? It is the struggle of one part of the people against another: the mass of the rightless, oppressed and toilers, versus the privileged oppressors and parasitic, the struggle of the workers or proletarians against the bourgeoisie owners. Turning that around demands strong conviction.

Bogdanov: And the solution: take from the haves and give to the have-nots?

Gorky: It is the eternal mirage.

Lenin: History notes often enough how the lower classes have risen up and tried to sweep away the hierarchical and qualitative differences in society, but class is quality and man is quantity. Class warfare elevated to an idea conceals the qualitative image of man, so that the idea of class kills the idea of man. Theoretically Marxian murder. The old always makes room for the new. It's the way of nature and governments. Life is dirty business.

Gorky: We all give up something along the way.

Lenin: We must delve deeper into that kind of thinking, which comes from nature herself. It's futile to resist change, which is like the turning of the seasons melting one into the other. Sooner or later one dominates and life moves on. No doubt, behind us another force is building to replace us. Our duty is get our ducks lined up properly. Our calling is to redistribute values, change thinking patterns, get people to understand the right way is not to covet to the detriment of others, but to share and nurture one another In this there is no room for selfish thought.

Gorky: Ilych, you sound like a priest.

Lenin: My God is of this world and justice is all the paradise I want. Bishop to Queen. Check.

Gorky: And I check you. Rrright!

Lenin: Chess is easier to play than life. Still, you must carry a lot in your noggin. Eh, Maxim? Checkmate.

Gorky: What? I had you cold. You cheated.

Lenin: Losers always think themselves cheated. It's how the mind works to keep its equilibrium, its sense of worth. Let's play cheater's chess. Same rules except if you're caught you lose.

Gorky: Bad government is like an unhealthy body where the finger tells the hand, the toes tell the foot, the heart refuses to pump because the blood says it is more important, the ass looks up and says, No. I'm more important than all of you. Without me you can't eliminate, a very important function. True. That's why people are such anal apertures.

Lenin: If the body acted the way governments act it would destroy itself. The body has an innate desire for homeostasis. Can't say that about government. What causes headaches?

Lunacharsky: Playing chess with you.

Lenin: A dog reflects its master. People reflect their government. The notion of kings and queens is delusional and destructive, breeds blind love, infantile adoration, and must be destroyed so people can grow up.

Gorky: Marya, what's for lunch?

Lenin: Eating is not conducive to writing and thinking. It satiates the appetite, dulls the senses, and brings on sleep. The white wolf bangs its head against the cage. Unlike other captives, it denies incarceration and keeps trying to find a way out. Something in the Russian character keeps banging away at chaos. We are happiest staring death in the face. We're all wolves gnawing at the same bone. (Marya starts waltz music.) The music changes, but the steps are the same. Three-quarter time for them, lentamente for the people. If fortune blesses me in my lifetime and the monarchy falls, I'll step onto a palace balcony, look out on the multitude, wave beneficently, and doubtless a young wolf will go, how'd he come so far in that shabby black suit with such a guttural "r"?

Gorky: How, indeed. (All dance; cross fade music to shrieking train whistle.)

ACT TWO

Scene 1: The Romanovs and Rasputin

Characters: Coachie; Mamushka; Tsar (Nicky); Tsarina (Sonny).
Place: The Grand Ballroom of Tsarkoe Selo

Coachie: (Dwn R.) Music, please. Blue Danube or Roses From the South, Op 388. (Music in.) That's The Emperor's Waltz. O, Roses is a medley. No matter. Good enough. The occasion is a dinner-ball for visiting foreign dignitaries in the grand ballroom at Tsarkoe Selo, the Winter Palace, as opposed to all the other seasonal palazzos. *It's my job, or rather, my tiresome duty, to introduce arriving nobility. Tfu! It's a living.* (Whistles.) A follow spot. (Spot on.) Over here, idiot! Spacebo. My crosier? Where's my? O, I'm holding it. How silly. Life can be like that, in your very hand and you don't even know it. Tfu! Frankly, as befits *the nobility*, I ought to walk out with pomp, trip, stomp the crook on my foot, scream bloody murder n' hobble about in pain. But why play the clown? There are plenty at court; more crooks than you can shake a buffoon at. And always the people cry, *are you serious? What's the joke?* (Enters formally, plays buffoon described above; recovers, bangs staff; shouts:) His royal heinouses, the Tsar, and Tsarina of Russia! (A butler's bell is heard; a bejeweled hand appears beckoning. HE goes to it, listens to the hand, returns, knocks staff, clears throat.) *Their* Royal Highnesses, the Tsar and Tsarina of *all the Russias!*

(MUSIC. Enter a pompous Tsar and Tsarina, aloof, and regal. He trips on her dress. They dance a snobbish waltz; dotted with sneers, fake compassion, contempt, and indifference with "veiled" vulgar gestures to the people. They swing around the floor, pause briefly Down C to speak.)

Tsarina: How many Russias are there, my pet?

Tsar: The sun never sets on us, my sparrow.

Tsarina: Ho hum. (Swinging around floor.)

Coachie: In its third year, the war with Germany goes poorly.

Tsarina: (Swinging by.) Pish posh.

Coachie: Russia verges on collapse—

Tsar: Nobody told me.

Tsarina: Vile rumors.

Coachie: The economy is down: There're shortages in food, fuel, and military supplies—

Tsar-Tsarina: O, fiddlesticks!

Coachie: Transportation is moving at a snail's pace.

Tsarina: I love escargot.

Coachie: Germany has exhausted Russia.

Tsar: Cousin Willy can bend your ear. (Swinging by.)

Coachie: The flower of Russian youth lays wasted in the mud of countless fronts.

Tsarina: Seditious gossip.

Coachie: Political exiles and deportees are called on to fight. One rifle for every ten men—

Tsarina: Fiddlesticks. Nicky has triple that in his hunting cabinet.

Tsar: More guns mean more money. What do you say, mon petite?

Tsarina: Increase the gun supply by reducing the ranks to half and it'll be one gun in five.

Tsar: Excellent! Ever the family brain, my little shrapnel.

Coachie: With an ammunition quota of 4 bullets a day.

Tsar: It only takes one to kill a man.

Coachie: Shoot five and the sixth one is for you.

Tsar: War's expensive. A line had to be drawn somewhere.

Coachie: The monarchy hangs by a thread. The streets are overrun with the jobless—

Tsarina: Get out of the street you won't get run over.

Coachie: Peasants are sleeping in gutters.

Tsarina: Tell them to go indoors. Bother, bother.

Coachie: Living in makeshift lean-tos, beggars everywhere shove filthy hands in your face begging for a kopek. The people have no bread.
Tsar: Let them eat caviar.
Tsarina: O, how clever! I've been thinking, Nicky.
Tsar: O, Sonny. Why? It upsets you so.
Tsarina: You should be more autocratic. Let them know who's boss.
Tsar: Take charge? O, but that's dangerous, my pet.
Tsarina: Just a thought.
Tsar: I'll sleep on it. (They whirl around and stop.)
Tsarina: Did your trip to the front go well?
Tsar: Wonderfully! Sitting on my white horse wearing my medals, I rallied the troops. Men! Give me victory! They go, Give us guns! I go, anything else? They go, Bullets to go with the guns!
Tsarina: Oh, that's funny. Boys and their toys. You didn't give in?
Tsar: No. I may be Tsar but I'm no fool. Bullets are rubles. We have a budget.
Tsarina: We do? How much? I'd like a new dress.
Tsar: There's the grand ball, dinner for the ambassadors and diplomats.
(They dance; stop.)
Tsarina: That horrid Rodzianko wants to call the Duma together to debate the war.
Tsar: Nobody told me.
Tsarina: Don't let him. It's not his business. Russia, thank God, is not a constitutional country.
Tsar: Not the last time I looked.
Tsarina: When was that?
Tsar: I can't remember.
Tsarina: It's better that way.
Tsar: I haven't looked since my coronation.
Tsarina: When was that?
Tsar: I can't remember.
Tsarina: *Gudt* for you, Nicky. Memory is a nuisance. Da.
Tsar: Say, that's Russian?
Tsarina: Ya. Es gudt, no?
Tsar: Est gudt, yes.
Tsarina: Been taking lessons, but I'm switching to French.

Tsar: Who can blame you?
Tsarina: Who'd dare? French is more civilized. After all, they invented the guillotine.
Tsar: Speaking of lessons. Look. A new step. (They whirl around.)
Tsarina: Wundabar, Nicky.
Tsar: Wundabar! How do you say that in Russian?
Tsarina: Forget it. It's a dead language, (Stops.) which reminds me. That horrible minister of censorship let an article go to press maligning 'our friend'—relating his latest debaucheries, peccadilloes and other distasteful matters. The censor failed in his duty. Fire him. Also, the Grand Duke's failure on the battlefield is intolerable.
Tsar: Set backs are bound to happen.
Tsarina: I don't like what he said about 'our friend'. He opposed Rasputin's request to visit the front and bless the troops.
Tsar: He did?
Tsarina: What does that oafish commander say? 'Come ahead and I'll hang you.' This, he said of 'our friend' who embodies the soul of Russia.
Tsar: I guess the Duke must go, too.
Tsarina: Indeed he must. Besides, he's becoming too well known. He might even be planning to displace you. Get rid of him before it's too late. You should be Commander-in-chief. You always loved military parades. Take command of the army. Do it. The people and soldiers love you.
Tsar: Think so? It's not just rumor?
Tsarina: They'd follow you without hesitation, to the end of the world.
Tsar-Tsarina: From God's lips to us!
(Enter Anna Vyubova with an urgent message.)
Anna: The Tsarevitch calls. (All bow; exit.)
(Stage R.)
Mamushka: They can't have been that out of touch.
Coachie: I'm kidding, but not by much.
Mamushka: You trying to sell me a wooden mug?
Coachie: No. They were babes in the woods like you said, "out of touch." The outrageous things the monarchy did: dismissing the

Duma, going to war ill equipped. It was so ludicrous one had to ask, What's the joke? The joke was black and it was on the people. If farmers ran farms the way politicians govern there'd be no food on the table. That day came, and all hell broke loose.

Mamushka: Aye-ya-ya! Between the cradle and the grave. Tfu! We get what we deserve. Yes, we do. Innocence in the wrong place. When growing up the Tsarina was such a nice princess, religious, beautiful, obedient, butter wouldn't melt in her mouth, but other than that—

Coachie: Superstitious.

Mamushka: So endearing.

Coachie: She hung back with totem poles, charm bracelets—

Mamushka: Other than that, genuine.

Coachie: She believed in mummies, voodoo spirits—

Mamushka: Other than that.

Coachie: A muddleheaded Hessian—

Mamushka: Incapable of deceit.

Coachie: With an autocratic Teutonic mind—

Mamushka: Other than that everything she did was in earnest.

Coachie: No feel for what it means to be Russian.

Mamushka: Ah, but then children play at throwing rocks at birds, yet the birds do not die in jest, but in earnest. Tfu!

Coachie: The real trouble began years before. They prayed for a male heir. Four girls popped out of the oven—

Mamushka: Quit that.

Coachie: Finally, a boy. They were jubilant. But soon discovered something was wrong, that something turned an empire upside down.

Cameo 1

(Natasha followed by Anna head for the service entrance to the Palace.)

Natasha: *Driver! Driver!* (Coachie steps up.) Take this note to the monk Rasputin. Hand it to him directly. Accept no go-betweens. Understood? If he is not at home, find him. Don't come back

without him. Bring him straightway to the servants' entrance. I'll be waiting. Go, go! Don't spare the horses, and don't come back without him. (HE goes.) He knows things, impossible things.
Anna: A dark animal, if you ask me. He gave me the shivers. The devil he is. Knotted hair, stiff beard, a sloping forehead, a broad nose. Mercy me.
Natasha: His eyes were extraordinary: a brilliant blue that sink to pinpoints, and change color like quicksilver. He cured me of my headache. I thought, maybe he can serve the Tsarevitch. He smelled like jasmine, or musk.
Anna: More like wet hay in a barn. It took courage to go in that room.
Natasha: I thought, what's to fear? He's a holy man. You should've been in there.
Anna: No thank you.
Natasha: His eyes were at once piercing and caressing, naïve and cunning, far off yet intense. I swear, his pupils radiated magnetism, lured and compelled me: glimmering eyes with an urgent, mysterious will behind them. I nearly swooned.
Anna: The man is offensive. Wonder what it would be like in his arms?
Natasha: They say a paramour shot him.
Anna: Mercy. The man's a sexual lightening rod.
Natasha: That goes without saying. But he's a monk, I thought, a holy man. What's to fear? First, he was kind, indulgent, and even fatherly then gradually his keen eyes bored into me down to my feet. My legs felt heavy like led. I had to sit. He sat next to me, edged closer, then his eyes changed color from light to dark blue. His bearded face, twisted into desire, moved close to mine, his hot breath on my cheeks, his eyes burning deep in their sockets, rolled over my body. His voice fell into a passionate whisper, voluptuous, sensual, and fascinating. I was at the point of abandonment, but something deep within me stirred, reminding me that I had come to him about God. I struggled free, gradually awoke. He sensed my resistance and stood up. His face full of desire became serene again, his voice benevolent, but in the depth of those beady eyes still lurked that other man, the sensual beast. I came away absolutely enthralled. (Lights down.)

Scene 2

(Lights up on the 7 year old Tsarevitch's candlelit bedroom; distant waltz music is heard. The boy has been bedridden for days suffering internal hemorrhaging. The doctors are stymied and death is immanent. The Tsarina prays at a kneeler; the Metropolitan concludes an orthodox blessing of everything and everyone, swinging an excessively smoky censor that chokes and brings tears to the eyes. The doctors two-step to avoid getting beaned. He exits blessing the audience, chasing away evil spirits. "Padre, Filgio, Spiritu, e Santo.")

Doctors: (*Hushed voices.*) Hot compresses. Cold! God, what's in that thing rotten eggs? Like to choke me to death. Alternate hot then cold. No. Cold then hot.
Tsarina: Dear God. Where have I failed? I search in vain for an answer, some weakness—
Tsar: He's a good boy.
Tsarina: Some act of omission.
Tsar: He'll make a fine Christian, Lord.
Tsarina: If I offended Thee, strike me not the child. Bring your discontent down on me, but spare my boy. I beg you with all my heart. Amen.
Tsar: (Turning to Empress.) Come, Sonny. Come, dearest.
Tsarina: Mm? What? How is he?
Tsar: Resting.
Tsarina: Thank God.
Tsar: Come. We have guests waiting.
Tsarina: Not just yet, dearest.

Tsar: Sonny, please. It will do you good. The French ambassador seemed eager to dance with you.
Tsarina: Oh, God, Nicky. I couldn't.
Tsar: At least return briefly, if you wish.
Tsarina: I haven't the heart.
Tsar: It is bad form to neglect guests.
Tsarina: Worse to neglect our son. Please, don't insist. I beg you. All my thoughts are here in this room with Alexeyva. I hear only his voice so small and helpless, full of pain. "Mother, mother, mother!" (Rises.) Is he calling now?
Tsar: No. He sleeps. Sonny, please. Guests when neglected begin thinking.
Tsarina: Don't you see? I'm rooted here. Tell them.
Tsar: It's better they know nothing. Come. The distraction will do you—
Tsarina: Distraction? (Rising.) I've heard nothing but one voice for days. Everything, everybody is off in another room. The orchestra plays, people talk, but I hear only one voice, a small innocent voice. It calls me now.
Tsar: He sleeps. Please, we have our duty—(Natasha appears in BG.)
Tsarina: Mine is here. I haven't the heart, Nicky. Please. Convey my regrets. Say I'm indisposed. Don't insist. If I leave, if something happens and I'm gone, how should I live with myself?
Tsar: As you wish, my dear.
Tsarina: A moment ago Nicholasha took hold of my finger, squeezed it in his little hand, pleading, Mamushka, when am I going to get better?
Tsar: For the love of God—
Tsarina: Yes, for the love of Him. To show His love this way—
Tsar: Careful. Dare you blaspheme—
Natasha: Excuse me, your majesty. (To Empress.) He is here, the monk.
Tsar: What monk?
Natasha: He comes at your invitation. Remember?
Tsar: A monk? The Metropolitan was just here.
Natasha: He's called the Holy Fool, a miracle man.

Tsar: Sonny, what is going on? You invited a monk into our home?
Tsarina: I don't believe I did that. Oh, yes—
Tsar: Why? Who is he? Has he a name?
Natasha: Starets, your majesty. All Petrograd is talking about him.
Tsar: Well, I'm not and I'm Russia.
Tsarina: It slipped my mind, Nicky. Let us see, try—
Tsar: Try what? The Metropolitan himself was here. There is no higher authority on earth. Right now he carries our indulgences to the church where he promises a thousand prayers. The clergy itself has been fasting. Good God, if he finds out he may take offense. What then if he's needed?
Tsarina: They say he has unsual powers, works miracles.
Tsar: The miracle is that I hold my patience.
Tsarina: I see none forthcoming from the Metropolitan.
Tsar: Watch your words. This is no time to—Send him away.
Tsarina: No, please. You speak of duty? What about your son? We have an obligation to him, to give him every chance to live. If he dies and we haven't tried everything, what then? Natasha, give us a minute and then show him in. (Natasha goes.) Thank you. I've reached the end of my rope, Nicky. Now we must be bold—
Tsar: Careful.
Tsarina: It cannot be the intention of God or the Church—
Tsar: Beware, beware! Would you circumvent God, too? Beware.
Tsarina: This monk is ordained, Nicky. We are still in the Church.
Tsar: But a low monk?
Tsarina: There is no heresy just the possibility of hurt pride. What is that compared to the life of our son? To deny the prayers of a monk because his position—
Tsar: Don't blaspheme.
Tsarina: My knees are worn to the bone. What next? Naked through the streets to the hot baths, flagellation, bang my head against stone? Mercy, God, Allah, Buddha!!
Tsar: Stop it, I say.
Tsarina: Alexis took hold of my finger—
Tsar: Don't.

Tsarina: Wrapped his hand around my finger squeezing the heart out of me. The pain in his eyes, his voice, Nicky.
Tsar: Please.
Tsarina: "Mother," he pleaded. "When am I going to get better?" I was speechless. Dumb as an ox. (Sardonic laugh.) How foolish life is, filling our heads with notions, I am Empress, you are Tsar, God has given us dominion over the greatest empire in the world. We lift a pinky, utter a syllable and our will is done, from God's lips to us, but from our lips to Him nothing. *When am I going to get better, mother?*
Tsar: Stop, I beg you.
Tsarina: *Mother, make the pain go away,* and I cannot. *But mother, you are the Empress; father is the Tsar.* Are we, Nicky, Empress and Tsar? If so, stop the bleeding. What has the child done to deserve this fate? He is innocent. I must be the guilty one. Yes. (Kneeling.) Tell me what to do, Lord. What have I done? Strike me dead, but spare my boy. (Pause.) There, you see? Nothing. We have everything and nothing. All our prayers and supplications are chaff in the wind. (Tsar turns away.) His eyes follow me, Nicky, into my dreams begging me: Mother, make the pain go away, and it repeats like a plaintive lyric. Make the pain go away. If we are significant and not meddlesome fools living some ghastly illusion, if our days are not a charade of conceit in a misbegotten monarchy then come forward, speak those magical kingly words for your son, lift your royal pinky, banish his suffering. I command you as Empress, wife, mother, human being. Do it!
(Tsar contains frustration. Enter Rasputin waltzing in frayed monk's robe, cowl, knotted black hair, long stiff beard. Sees the Empress; licks his lips.)
Rasputin: God tempts me yet again. This time with birds in a gilded cage, I in my temporal one. And it's such fun! To stick your nose in people's affairs. Try living in a monastery. Bore the shit out of you. Ah, ooh, the place smells of the begging bowl. (Chuckling.) Fashionable dolts! Ha. The bitch wants something. Everybody wants something even the rich. What a delicious prospect, mother love. Sweeter even, mother's milk. And delectable, too. I almost wish I'd bathed. No. Repugnance is one of my main attractions. Ha. Better she should speak to Lucifer than Rasputin. Tfu! Plain as

the face on your nose. Me, me, me. Gimme, gimme gimme. Pain, like laughter and tears, speaks with one voice. How far will she go? We shall see. Burn Russia to save the child. Why not? What is Russia to a nemka? O. Here comes the big baba bull.

Tsar: Step forward.

Rasputin: I am forward, so they say, or do you prefer I come in backwards.

Tsar: What's that?

Rasputin: Yes, sire. Whatever pleases you. Though irreverent in my reverence, I bow in reverence. (Bowing.) Rasputin, at your service.

Tsar: A monk and you call yourself Rasputin?

Rasputin: (Inclines head.) Mm, yes.

Tsar: An odd name for a holy man.

Rasputin: I bare the name as penance for a former life. Yet if a Rasputin pulls thee from certain death, is he then dissolute or Jesus Christ, your savior? How may I serve you?

Tsarina: The Tsarevitch is very ill.

Rasputin: Bleeds.

Tsarina: Yes. The doctors tried everything—

Rasputin: Have they tried leaving? There is too much fretting and tension in the air thick as a bog. Send them away. They make me nervous I cannot work when I am nervous.

Tsar: What work is that?

Rasputin: God's work. He commands. I obey. I am his puny emissary, his performing monkey.

Tsar: What rubbish.

Rasputin: That's it. He grinds out His rubbish, I dance, a power comes over me, and *Things* happen.

Tsar: What things?

Rasputin: Miracle things, I am told. Who can presume to explain God in his wisdom, or why He chose me? As you see from my name, I am the last person you would expect to be His confidant.

Tsar: God speaks to you?

Rasputin: He talks to everybody in different ways. Most people don't know how to listen. They're too busy talking. He speaks through impulse, urges, and intuition. Even now He speaks. Do you hear Him?

Tsar: All I hear is your nonsense.
Rasputin: Then permit me to say you're not truly listening. Listen. It's the boy, yes? He bleeds. Yes? How do I know? Nothing happens by accident. He led me here for a reason. He has His ways. Here I am at your service. Accept me, accept Him. Temporal reasons I leave to others. They are still here, them, those frauds. They make me nervous, your majesties. You and they hang too much over the child. He senses their confusion and your anguish, fears and doubts; and it disturbs him. Get them out. Nobody touches the boy but Rasputin.
(Tsarina dismisses doctors; Rasputin approaches bed cautiously, and proceeds with nonsense syllables and cadences of fairy tale words.)
Tsarevitch: (Weakly.) Mamenka, the sheet hurts my knee.
Rasputin: (Draws closer.) Now batyushka (little father) is here. Even shpyukin (Postman) . . . da . . . comes on a flying stove—Na palatyakh—sitting on the shelves, a pot for a hat, a spoon for a nose, gold thimble eyes, ears like big bliny, cherry lips, a samovar belly, and pockets of shchi to warm your belly. I'll tell you a secret. Promise not to tell anybody. When it thunders it's the angels bowling with cabbages. Da. Slava Bohu! Have no fear. No worries. Look into my eyes. My eyes are with you always. Say it. All-ways. (Tsarevitch weakly: "All-ways." Sonny steps forward; the Tsar mutters: "This is absurd." Rasputin waves them back, leans into the boy's face.) The pain is going away, slowly going away, and my little pirate boy is sailing in a pumpkin on a sea of borscht, the wind at your back. You fly along, a purple parrot on your shoulder. O, little pirate boy, how beautiful you are, full and bright as the morning star. Nothing can hurt or harm you. Nothing. Say it. Nothing.
Tsarevitch: Nothing.
Rasputin: The stars are holes in the sky through which His light shines down to watch over us at night. HE sees everything and everybody, every creature that walks the earth. Some make Him happy, some make him sad. You make Him sad. He wants you to get better, to run and play, and asked me to tell you "fear not." In me God is with you. He heals those who want healing. Do you want to be healed? (Tsarevitch nods weakly.) Then His will be

done. You are God's gift to the world. Such a beautiful gift, one that knows only joy and happiness, and running in the fields. The moon is your kite, big and golden with a long red tail, longer than the tongues of five hundred dragons and two turkeys. Now you are strong, so strong that nothing can hurt you. Trust Rasputin. Not your finger, not your leg. Nothing. Da?

Tsarevitch: Da.

Rasputin: Little boy pirate is strong, stronger than the little ant that lifts twice, three times its weight and carries it off to build its nest or the bee that travels a hundred versts, but always comes home. How do they do it? Magic. The entire world is a zakuski of magic. Da. Ty, ty, believe with all your heart in the magic of Moo-jee-ga-loo-jee. Ha, ha. Say it. Moo-jee-ga-loo-jee.

Tsarevitch: Moo-jee—

Rasputin: Galoo-gee.

Tsarvitch: Moo-jee-galoo-jee.

Rasputin: Look into my eyes. Deep, deep. The pain has left you and is in my eyes. You no longer feel pain. It is far away, higher than the kite, beyond the moon far away. So far away that it can't touch you. Gone completely away; and now you will sleep; and when you wake up you will be rested, and happy, and content. Sleep, sleep. Moo-jee-ga-loo-jee . . . (Lights fade out.)

Scene 3:
Death of A Holy Fool and A Monarchy

Time: 1915-1916.
Place: St. Petersburg.
Characters: Mamushka; Coachie, plays Vasily; Prince Felix Yusupov, Vladimir Pureshkevich, resolved; Grand Duke Boris Pavlovich, ex court minister, bachelor, nephew of Alex III; Dr. Vasily, fearful; Two soldiers.

Coachie: O, there are several versions.
Mamushka: What is yours?
Coachie: Hearsay mostly: poison, gunshot, drowned, maybe all three. The man wasn't normal. Stepping back a little . . . Rasputin's growing influence and meddling at court, and then horrified hearing in the summer of 1915 that the Tsar was planning to take over the army disgusted the Tsar's Cabinet Ministers.
Ministers: (Passing by.) Imagine Woodrow Wilson of the United States leading his army? Or King George V of England taking command of his fleet in the middle of war? Ha! The very idea is absurd. The man's got a full plate just leading the country. Good Lord. If he fails at the front it'd be disaster. Then what's to stop the Tsarina and Rasputin from taking over the government?
Coachie: A moot question. They already had. The Tsar was torn between the Tsarina whispering in his ear and his cabinet ministers each pulling him in different directions. On September

3rd the royal couple showed up at three different churches, prayed before various icons; and the next day he went to the front, relieved the Grand Duke his uncle, reassigned him to the Caucasus, and set himself up as commander-in-chief headquartered at Mogilev on the Dneiper. When the news reached his cousin Kaiser Willy he doubled over laughing and couldn't wait to attack with a couple of tanks just to see what cousin Nicky would do. At home the top bureaucratic ministers were replaced by a succession of Rasputin appointees. Frankly, I think there were domestic problems at the palace. Think on it: a naïve superstitious wife who believed in mystics and mummies, a crazy mystagogue drug addict monk, five active kids—one a hemophiliac whose every move was a thousand frights should he fall, bruise himself, bleed. Who wouldn't want to get out of the house, palace or no palace? To the Tsar war was a vacation. At the front, he pranced about in uniform, chest emblazoned with phony medals, blue eyes sparkling in the sunlight—glad to be free of the political intrigue at home, the courtiers, and corrupt ministers. Defeats at the front and Rasputin's shenanigans at home strengthened the revolutionaries on the right and left. There were strikes. Soldiers refused to fire on the workers. Cossacks had to restore peace. Under the syphilitic Sturmer, president of the council of ministers, 150 mutinous soldiers were shot. Meanwhile, a Brigade of Russians rebelled in France against its officers. The French shot the mutineers. In the monarchist drawing rooms they talked openly of deposing the Tsar in favor of his son with the Grand Duke as regent. The Duma was for it and set to meet. The Empress wrote the Tsar. *How I wish I could hang that Rodzianko,* and claimed Sturmer was a German spy. Then Milyukov the Kadet leader favoring a constitutional monarchy and no revolutionary, attacked Rasputin, listing charges against the government, "Is This Folly or Treason?" Seditious talk was on everyone's mind, but few dared to speak openly. The Tsarina had only one worry: that the Tsar might weaken. In December 1916 the Empress wrote the Tsar:

Cameo 1 (At her writing desk.)

Tsarina: *Russia loves to feel the whip. O, Nicky, how I wish I could pour my will into your veins. I've had no sleep; but listen to me, which means 'Our Friend'. I suffer over you as over a tender softhearted child. Pardon, believe, and understand. I have a plan to deport the political party leaders to Siberia. Be the Emperor. Be Peter the Great, John the Terrible—crush them all. God has placed us on the throne. We must keep it firm and give it over to our son untouched. I kiss you, caress you, love you, long for you, can't sleep without you, and bless you. Don't yield an inch, my dearest. Be the boss. Obey your firm little love-dove, and 'our friend'. Believe in us.*

Mamushka: I've been thinking three things that have repeatedly come to mind: he was a man of his time, his heart's in the right place, and accountability. What do you think they mean?
Coachie: He was a victim of circumstance, destroyed lives, murdered millions, but meant well!
Mamushka: You went along with it? Tfu!
Coachie: Well, don't shoot me for them, or go ahead and shoot. It's all the same to me. Here today, gone tomorrow. I'll be glad when I'm gone.
Mamushka: Self-pity doesn't become you. Get on with it.
Coachie: The Bolsheviks' first priority on resting control of the government was *quit the war with Germany and build a socialist state.* Who were Russia's allies anyway? Did they have a special love for Russia? To the West we were merely a tool for *Détente,* a balance of power. The British and French were ready to fight to the last Russian. What did the Tsar think at the time, or his Hessian wife? She adopted with a kind of cold fury traditions and nuances of Russian medievalism, the most meager and crude of all medievalism, in that very period when the people were making mighty efforts to free themselves from it. This Hessian princess was literally possessed by the demon of autocracy. Having risen from her rural corner to the heights of Byzantine despotism, she would not for anything take a step down. Wine improves with age, not so

the Romanovs. They merely sunk lower and lower until the people burst the seams of their pent up anger and went wild. Toward the end of 1916 Russia had been at war with Germany three long hard years. *Then Vladimir Pureshkevich spoke out in the Duma against Rasputin. Listening in the public gallery was a young nobleman, Prince Felix Yusupov. What he heard affected him deeply. He set his mind to saving Russia.* Trepov the new Prime Minister tried to buy off Rasputin: a hundred thousand dollars cash, a house and living expenses providing he kept out of politics, plus, free reign over the clergy. Rasputin laughed it off. So here we are late December 1916. Winter's been hard—the sort that turns one's mood to despair and melancholy: soldiers deserting by the thousands, the prospect of victory dim, food is scarce, and an immanent threat of Zeppelins hangs heavy, the cold bone deep, the monarchy on the brink of collapse. The Parliament hates the bureaucracy. The bureaucracy hates parliament. The Tsarina hates parliament, the bureaucracy, and everything in between. On top of that Rasputin is holding court like a devil in God's name and getting away with it. Tfu! His arrival on the scene made matters worse. Rasputin was running the government to the abhorrence of even the most corrupt and sycophantic court ministers. Rasputin moved about Petrograd in grandiose style, holding court in his apartment suite like a pasha, tending the rich and the poor, giving jobs to the husbands of wives who slept in his bed. Those who refused him he'd have their husbands fired. Charlatans and scoundrel priests he'd chosen held church offices. Everyone feared Rasputin. He could break anyone over night. In 1916 several men from the nobility conspired to act. They were not happy with the Tsar, but pro-monarchists and for the status quo which meant continued oppression of the people, continued deceit and self-aggrandizing by corrupt officials. The "lie", as is, was ok with them. While Rasputin was against the war, he waged one inside the government by destroying the ministers' illusion of exclusivity. Well, the whole thing was a black joke, a tragic-comedy waiting in the wings, one worthy of the Greeks, but in the end turned into a cheap moving picture scenario designed for people of bad taste. Come. Wipe your feet at the door. Let's look in.

Cameo 2:

Rasputin's Quarters

(A drunken-drugged Rasputin primps as Felix looks on with disguised impatience and drunkenness. Rasputin picks up a gift from a stack, opens it, throws away the gift, and admires the wrapping.)

Rasputin: (Bragging.) Twenty-one ministers, by God! Out! Out! Gave 'em a doss of their own medicine! Dispatched 'em all with wonderful brutality. No more than they deserve. What's good for the goose? Hand me that bottle. Not that one. Idiot! The blue. One I drink the other I wear. (Sprays self and Felix.) Tastes better than it smells.
Felix: Phew!
Rasputin: The only good thing about an Oxford education you learn to lie in many languages.
Felix: To lie in French mitigates the sting. Frankly, I prefer Latin. It's lean and militaristic.
Rasputin: This is Latin, (Sprays him.) from an Italian princess—a slip of a child. Have some more. Repulsive, yes, but not her. Ha! Stinks, eh? But not half as bad as the stench of nobility.
(Felix backs away pursued by Rasputin. Lights down, up on:)

Scene 4:
Upstairs Parlor, Yusupov Palace

Pureshkevich: Nothing wrong with revolution. A little change now and then reinvigorates the blood.
Vasily: Better a steam bath than this.
Pureshkevich: New blood replaces old blood.
Vasily: Ghastly business.
Pureshkevich: New life pushes out old life. So it is, has ever been, even in the realm of ideas: To everything there is a time, a time to live and a time to die.
Boris: (By the stairs door.) It's them. Wait. No. Just a cat.
Pureshkevich: Sometimes life has to be forced, pushed to the brink, helped along to do in a minute what nature would do in years. Who can say that what we do this night is not nature's plan of purgation?
Vasily: A fine word for murder.
Pureshkevich: I rather like it myself. I take a purgative now and then to rid myself of toxins. Afterward, I feel renewed and can't wait to get laid.
Vasily: Is that your plan after this filthy business?
Boris: Somebody's getting fucked tonight.
Pureshkevich: For what we do this night all Russia will bless us, kiss the cross, and dance. You can only invoke God's name to cover evils but so many times before the truth strangles you.
Vasily: Where the devil are they? Maybe he knows and the police—

Pureshkevich: Everything's set? Vasily! (Vasily nods.) Poisoned cakes, wine? Good. Remember to keep playing that record. He must believe the duchess is with guests wining, dining, and dancing.
Vasily: Christ! I don't know how to dance.
Boris: Just shuffle your feet, move like this. Laugh, dance for Russia.
Pureshkevich: But don't forget our purpose.
Vasily: Forget? It's eating me alive.
Pureshkevich: Think of it as filial love.
Vasily: God! You politicians can talk around anything,—purgation, love. It's detestable business plain and simple.
Pureshkevich: We're saving Mother Russia from a beast at her breast sucking her blood dry for years. (Noises off.) It's them. They're here.
Vasily: O, God! I feel nauseous.
Pureshkevich: Get back, y'fool.
Vasily: I'm going to throw up.
Pureshkevich: You'll give us away. Quick. Start the music. The snare tightens, and with it our resolve. (Vasily retches.) Beast or man we'll soon know.

Scene 5

(Basement, Yusupov Palace, Ante room to the wine cellar; fireplace, couch, low table, rug, candles, standing cross; expensive wine bottles; poisoned sweet cakes. Rasputin trips on entering; recovers.)

Rasputin: Like a cat with nine lives. Indestructible! God said, *let there be light*, but missed this fuckin' place, or have I gone blind? Lights! (Felix turns on sconces.) Yee gads, a wino's paradise.
Felix: Father's joy, mere samplings of what is beyond in the wine cellar.
Rasputin: The barracks! Here these good soldiers wait to die. They're not squeamish?
Felix: Stalwart and at your service.
Rasputin: Call them to duty. (Trumpeting.) Tar-rah! (Grabs two bottles.) Reporting for duty, sir! At your service, sir!
Felix: A coterie blend of near and far loyalists. (Picks up bottles.) One gets drunk saying the names. Reporting for duty, sir! Yes, sir!
Rasputin: Where you from, soldier?
Felix: Saigogne Burgogne, sir! Bordeaux, Sir! Aligote Margaux, Crois de la Gay, sir! Beaujolais, Volnay, Maconnais, Cote d'Or, Cote Chalomaise, sir! Choosing can be difficult.
Rasputin: Not for a peasant. It's water with or without chicken shit. This fellow was on the front line. (Taking up a bottle.)
Felix: Called up today before coming to you. (Pours wine, hands glass to Rasputin who drinks.) No, no, mon ami. Slowly, slowly. Good wine must be savored like a good woman, come ça. (Pores a

glass; swirls it round, sniffs it.) Lies brilliant in the glass; you feel first le fragrance. Then sip it for the palate to—

Rasputin: What palate? (Starts to drink.)

Felix: No, no. Sniff it, mon ami. Savor it. Come ça, come ça. (Drinks a little.) An interesting bouquet, fruity, not bitter, with a touch of oak. A good wine holds its quality after being opened. (Hands glass to Rasputin.) Let the wine move around the glass, and then nose it. Take in the bouquet. It's a young wine.

Rasputin: This bitch talks back. I don't like it. You got Madeira?

Felix: Qui, qui. Portugal. Some days deciding on what to drink can be so trying. What goes with meat, what goes with fish, the vintage-?

Rasputin: I drink water. Goes with everything. You can tell the vintage by the rust. Let it settle and drink. Where's the Madeira?

Felix: Eeny, meeny miney moe. Over there. O, my, which way to go! Decisions. Apple, Honey, Almond, o, this one's a favorite of the duchess, the name rolls off the tongue, the wine goes down smoothly, Puilly Fuisse from Lyons, no, no, Burgogne with a black Current flavor. Cote de Beaune, Cote d'Or, Cote de Nuit—

Rasputin: Coat my tongue with a Madeira, goddamnit! I'm dry.

Felix: See? Just the names excite the palate. Pick one: Chateaux Margeau, Clos de la Roche, Burgundy Red, Beaujolais Blanche.

Rasputin: What the hell is this?

Felix: The widow, Veuve Clicquot. Excellent. Quite rare. There's Chateau Lafite from Bordeaux. Next to it is a Chasagagne, Montrachet south of the Cote de Beaune. Simple not complex. This one's a deep red—

Rasputin: The blood of Christ!

Felix: You lived in a monastery. The monks were first to cultivate grapes.

Rasputin: And each other. The hypocrites. Tfu! They don't admit it, but they love the grape. I used to annoy them. I'd go, (Singing.) *Did God set grapes growing, you think, only to make it a sin to drink? Give thanks to Him for he loves to hear the glasses clink.* What got the poor bastards through the cold night?

Felix: (Takes up guitar.) The blessed grape.

Felix and Rasputin: (Singing.) Da. The blood of Christ. *Did God set grapes a-growing, y'think, only to make it a sin to drink? Give thanks to Him for he loves to hear the glasses clink.* (Repeat.)
Rasputin: What else was there to do in those cold bleak stone fortresses? Nothing, I can tell you. The grape became salvation, eased doubts and fears. At night the fucking shadows in those chilly stone halls were enough to make you crazy. Achtungt! At your command, sir! What do you call these Frenchies?
Felix: In your right is a Clos de la Roche, vintage, 1890; and your left a Criot Batard Montrachet Grand Cru, vintage, 1905.
Rasputin: Cossacks ready for duty.
Felix: Certainment. S'accomodi.
Rasputin: It's a comedy all right. Blood of Christ. It's blood of the people.
Felix: There. There is your vintage Madeira.
Rasputin: By God, you know how to treat a man. (Opens bottle, drinks.)
Felix: Tre gauche.
Rasputin: Shut up, will you?
Felix: Slowly. It wants to breathe. Been bottled up since 1890.
Rasputin: By God! Ahh! The bouquet is complex, not bitter, a slight taste of oak maybe. (Drinks.) Yes. A hint of Oak with a touch of urine. Goat piss! Tre good, Felix. Bring on the rest. Let's drink the joint dry. What do you say? I'll bet you wipe your ass with vintage rose water. Ha! The Tsarina has powdered toilet paper. Do you?
Felix: Naturalment. The good life is the best life. Why settle for less? For anyone who feels, life is tragic; and for those who think, it's a joke. My bet noire? I feel and I think.
Rasputin: And drink. You should be more temperate like me. Ha, ha! My heart bleeds for your rich ass. Now cut the shit! Sing! Play!
Felix: (Strums; sings.) Un chanson—
Rasputin: Any fuckin' thing.
Felix: O, come with me, mon ami, on a winged troika to Normandy; Cote d'Azure, here wine's the cure; Chassagne Beaujolais, Cote di Beaune Merlot Cabernet; The valley of Loire, vin rouge o bianche, drink, sing e voila! E voila! E voila! Ici la Provence un baguette

gruyere por vous, avec Criot Batard Montrachet Gran' Cru. Say, this St. Pete o Cote de Nuit? No, mon petite, c'est la Chateau Lafite. E voila! E voila! A toast to the Tsar n' caviar, avec un bon Pinot Rouge c'est soir.

Rasputin: Play a gypsy song and dance. Hey! Ha! Ayah! (Dances; flings bottle against wall.)

Felix: Good for you! Not that one. No, no. (Rasputin tosses another.) O, what the hell! (Tosses bottle.) To Germany! Germans shoot bullets, but French throw wine. Let the walls drink, too.

Rasputin: Why not? They support your dead ass night and day. (Throws bottle.) Felix, you should be a monk.

Felix: I am a skunk.

Rasputin: Exactly. You'll get away with even more shit.

Felix: Like the decisions you plant in the Tsarina's ear?

Rasputin: Not me. God decides. I obey. (Drinks.) I take a steam bath at night; drink several bottles of Madeira before planning a course of action.

Felix: You, not God?

Rasputin: Who can say? His will works in mysterious ways. When I have a difficult problem I write it down on paper, stick it under my pillow; sleep on it, and in the morning I proclaim, "Rasputin has decided. My will prevails." Then I tell the Tsarina my decision, and she tells the Tsar. Other times I drop suggestions around like wood chips flying from an axe. Later, she makes a decision thinking it was her own. All by slight of mind, deary. Monkey Doodle went to town riding a droshky-What rhymes with droshky?

Felix: Write it on a piece of paper and sleep on it.

Rasputin: Careful I don't write your name down. Ha, ha.

Felix: Droshky, Tchaikovsky.

Rasputin: That Oxford education paid off, my fine-feathered fop. (Dancing.) Idiot bonehead cabinet ministers. Dry leaves. I'm the ointment in their fly.

Felix: It's the other way around.

Rasputin: Either way they itch my ass! We drinking or talking?

Felix: Help yourself. Un moment. Grandfather's balls. Hickory dickory dock the mouse ran up the clock. Wait. Listen. (Points to clock.) One, two, three, voila! (Clock strikes nine.)

Rasputin: Where the hell's that duchess? Woman! Rasputin is waiting! Get your ass down here! Phay-lix, you gave me an idea. I'm donating my balls to the church as bell knockers. Every day they'll sound matins, the angelus, and whenever a nun gets a poke in the bun. Are you Fey-lix or Phal-lics? God! Is this a room or a toilet? Feels like a cave. That gives me another idea, Phal-lics. Fucking like a bat in a cave, yes, hanging upside down. Do bats screw upside down? People do, but not while hanging. We're all bats anyway. Verkh nogame! (*Upside down*). Eh?

Felix: Sure. Just don't let go.

Rasputin: Yusupov, that's Polish. No. Mongolian. Maybe from Ghenkis Khan. Ach! Smes! Verkh nogame. (*Life's mixed, upside down.*) Ah, there you are (*Pointing to wine.*), standing tall at attention like a good Cossack sentinal ready for duty. Yes, your majesty, sir! Ready and able, your majesty, sir. (Drinks.) Ruby blood of Christ! To Jesus! To Joseph! (Drinks.) To Virgin Mary! (Drinks.) Nasdrovia! People want to kill me. Let 'em. I'd rather die young than end like those old bastard courtiers, dried leaves on a dead tree. Ahh! (Drinks.) I had a nun once with Himalayan breasts. She told me, I don't do that sort of thing. No exceptions. Her skin white as snow, her molten blood. She wasn't even a virgin. How do y' like that? Jesus snuck in somewhere.

Felix: You know where nuns go when they die? To Peter and *Ball*.

Rasputin: Vulgarity in the presence of a monk. Shame on you, Phay-lics of Oxford.

Felix: Your umbrage is out of character.

Rasputin: My roughness is no invitation for others to play down to me. While familiarity breeds contempt one should know their place and watch their tongue. If you think a palace and servants are no match for a bowl and cowl, wrong, dreary. You were born in the lap of luxury which destroyed your essence. You've become your clothes. The bowl and cowl becomes me because they're a poor man's way of begging food with dignity. Now others beg me, *Stay; don't go.* I oblige for a price. Those who pay, ride. Those who don't, walk. I've been thrown out of more villages. God, this is awful! (Tosses glass.) God's blood turned to piss. Phay-lics, let's go to the gypsies. They know how to treat a man. Pha-lics, you should be a monk.

Felix: Me, celebate?

Rasputin: There's no end to what you can get away with in the name of God. I bless the wenches n' anoint them with my crosier. Lately, I have no desire to become an old grape on a vine: juiceless, shriveled up left for birds to peck at. When it comes to that, shoot me.

Felix: I may shoot you anyway. (Points guitar at him; plucks string.)

Rapustin: (Fakes being shot.) O! I die! Et tu, Brute! Ahhh, I kick them all in the ass. (Goes to statue) Boo! Same to you, stone bitch. Where are your clothes, mamushka? Eh? (Caresses statue.) Mm, very nice. Tonight, Felix my noble shit, I like you even more than usual. (To statue.) You were flesh and blood once, mamushka. You lusted. Your loins were hot. What turned you to stone? Ah, the slights of youth. Youth is everything. Sweet innocence in a supple body, passion quivering just below the surface ready to explode at the slightest touch. Or were you always a cold bitch? Jesus lusted. His second coming was better than the first. Christ has risen! Where? Here! (Grabs crotch.) Phallics, the duchess.

Felix: In a minute.

Rasputin: Look at Him. (Pointing to cross.) Poor bastard's been hanging two thousand years.

Felix: Long enough, eh, mon ami?

Rasputin: He admonished us and was crucified. A lesson in what it means to tell the truth. Now we pray to him for salvation with psalms, hymns, and pageants. He came down to us, but we have yet to come up to him. I feel like splitting a silver birch for Jesus! I'm dry as a bone.

Felix: Have a sweet cake. Baked them myself.

Rasputin: The hell you did? Another Cossack ready for duty. Let's see. (Takes bottle.) On duty since the Tsar ascended the potty in 1812.

Felix: They improve with age. Here is a youngster 1898.

Rasputin: Yes, sir! (Drinks.) Your royal majesty, sir! (Tosses bottle.)

Felix: "Once more," dear fellow, "into the breech! . . . My kingdom for a horse." Better a Beaujolais.
Rasputin: Y'know what you fear most?
Felix: Yes. Something you'll say that will make me think.
Rasputin: When I say you, I mean the nobility. You fear the masses might rise up and kill you in your bed. (Tosses a bottle.)
Felix: Absolutely. That is why we build palaces with high walls.
Rasputin: In knowing that you wrong the people comes your fear of them. You'd be lost without the narodniki your canon fodder and all around jackasses who sweat blood to support your arrogant, spendthrift lifestyle. Educate them—
Felix: God forbid!
Rasputin: You'd have to wipe your own ass.
Felix: Frankly, I've forgotten how.
Rasputin: Who built this stone city where the northern frost cracks your bones? The people, the people built Peter, y'noble shit. They even build the gallows on which you hang them for demanding their rights. For all their toil what has been their compensation? Life in a mud hut, the yolk and whip, hunger and sickness punctuated by a periodic circus of war in the name of some fraudulent common boogieman—Poland, Ukraine, and now Germany. Rubbish and rot! (Drinks.) Ach, vinegar!
Felix: Wine like people can turn. To the Kaiser and Germania. Go to the devil! (Tosses bottles.) We're out of ammunition, but not wine. Nasdrovia!
Rasputin: A secret, Phal-lics. The only time I feel close to Him—
Felix: The devil or Him with a capital H?
Rasputin: Two sides of the same coin. I'm closest to God when I'm fucking some bitch. I told the Metropolitan, and the phony bastard faked blushing. Who knows how many virginal sisters he anointed with his crosier? From aoul to asshole. As I confessed my sins with women, I think the old guy was masturbating. Da. He kept saying, *kindly repeat that more slowly, my son.* Well, what the hell else has he got in the monastic life? They praise God with a lot of self-indulgence, I can tell you. Funny. We're born and the first thing we do is cry. Instinctively, we know this is a bad place. I confess I transgress, do penance, fast, and then repeat the whole damn thing over again. Were it not for wine and sex life would be

a horror. Then Jesus shows up and turns procreation into guilt. (Drinks.) A fine fix, eh? Why? You're educated. Why?

Felix: Greed n' envy, my friend. Cannibalism repressed into deportment.

Rasputin: Sexual affliction and benediction. You wenches, here is my bene-diction. Tell you another secret.

Felix: Two? This is my lucky day.

Rasputin: (Eats a cake.) Mm! A peculiar taste. (Eats.) Ah, pistachio.

Felix: Actually, I lied. The duchess made them for you.

Rasputin: She's not looking to get married, is she? Well, here's a secret. This afternoon a princess came to me, very young and fetching, and most delectable. Poor thing was suffering. From what she couldn't say, but I knew. She says, *Perhaps it's a malaise.* I go, *Such a fancy name for a common ailment.* She says, *Common? How so?* Then I move in, *You tire of innocence. You see, innocence becomes you, my dear. The glory of your unsullied vulva, between the mountains of your thighs lays the hair of the village dog, straining at the leash.* She says, *Have you remedy to relieve my may-laise?* So, tout suite I gave her my bene-diction! If only her father, some archduke, could've seen his darling princess prim and proper, screaming and twisting. Ha. Become a monk. The shit you get away with. You know him very well. No matter. Funny, the more I drink the drier I feel. The more I pray the more impassioned I get. Very odd. There's a good soldier. (Pours drink; turns bottle on its side.) A dead soldier. Call up another from the ranks for duty! (Salutes bottle; Felix puts new bottle on table.) Jesus said, *This bread is my body, eat. This wine is my blood. Drink of it.*

Here's to Jesus. Without Him lots of bums'd be out of work. Nasdrovia! (Drinks; flops onto couch.) God's a gargoyle in my gut: loveable, repulsive, mercurial, shameless, flagellant, sweet beast of death dancing here, there, East, West. Russia, Germany. Watch me dance! Hey-yah! (Collapses.) Russia's God's idiot, sinful, repentant, lost between burning sand and bone crushing winter. Here's to Peter The Great, and his rock Petrograd. Nosdrovia! (Nods off; mumbles.) Catherine The Whore. Ivan The Terrible, the Romanovs and their bloody bleeder. Without him I'd be the Metropolitan's footstool. Tfu! (At the cross.) God. Speak to this wretched carnivore. (Kisses cross.) Your ass is cold. To hell with her! I go to the gypsies. There you can unload everything for a price, and you know where you stand. (Stumbles onto couch in drowsy state; Felix watches him for signs of collapse. Rasputin drifts in and out of consciousness; belches.) I hate church music. Ahh! (Belches.) I've had my appetizer. Where's the main course, idiot?

Felix: When the bait is strong, anticipation overrides caution and the hunter unaware becomes prey.

Rasputin: What's that?

Felix: How do you make a woman's will your own?

Rasputin: Tibetan herbs and what they are too proper to acknowledge. They want to fornicate; feel life, the lash, and I give it to them. Virgins kneel at my feet, innocent, trusting. The fools! I'll tell you secret. Sex is stronger than religion. It's power. Blinding and unquestioned power.

Felix: That cross was a gift from Tolstoy who was fond of my grandfather, but gran'pa never reciprocated that affection. He refused it, but Tolstoy never picked it up. Too busy, I suspect, planting on his farm.

Rasputin: Planting what, his foreskin?

Felix: How common you are.

Rasputin: What?

Felix: I said, how quaint you are. Gran'pa was not given to poetics. He was a realist, very direct, a character trait I didn't inherit. But I play guitar, sing, and spend money so well—a natural gift, I guess. Everyday I wake up and say, how shall I spend money today? Money decisions can be difficult when you have everything. Tolstoy had the same problem. So he gave it all away. Well, it was his to give. Mine is not mine yet, but belongs to father. I doubt I'll give it away. Spend it, yes. Have a sweet cake, mon ami. Life is such a challenge. Still, I don't relish bankrupting the family. Ha. I don't think it's possible.

Rasputin: I've never had a kopek myself, but I've a talent for distributing other people's money. There are so many ways. I have yet to exhaust them all. That's why I meddle in government. The sky's the limit. Each of us in our way keeps the economy rolling. Tfu! What do you say we roll out of here to the gypsies?

Felix: Here. (Hands him a bottle.) A gift. Call it my largesse.
Rasputin: Keep your large ass. Speak to me in cash.
Felix: (Tosses him a pouch.) There. Enough for, well, who knows, a minute, a day, a week? I am the rich man's Tolstoy. C'est la vie. Tolstoy was passive, a dreamer. My grandfather was active, privy to decisions. *True aesthetics,* he told Tolstoy, *are deeds, not words, in men's actions. What men do is art in action: the beauty and horror of spontaneous confrontation, the blood and guts of the moment, the sword descending with far reaching consequences. These are materials of the prima facie artiste, the pen but a weak sister.* One Christmas Tolstoy arrived in peasant's clothes, yelled up from the entrance begging gran'pa to join him at midnight Mass. Gran'pa declined, saying he had family business. Besides, he mistrusted artists, thought them irresponsible, whimsical. Soon after, Tolstoy denounced the state-directed orthodox Church; renounced the glittering aristocratic life; gave away his city home, his belongings; gave up his title of count; and the glittering aristocratic life, retiring to his *smaller* estate in the country, an ancestral farm; exalted manual labor, plowing, harrowing, planting with the muzhiks.
Rasputin: He in his farmhouse. They in their mud huts. Life's sad poetry. What can he know of the farmer's troubles: the earth gone barren, too much rain, too little rain, insects, a bad crop? These things are born in the bones from the womb. That's everything, isn't it? What's born in the bones. He felt the people's pain which you sweep under the carpet. Play something folksy. Pluck up a gypsy song with those manicured fingers.
Felix: How about the Red Dress, or a dance tempo?
Rasputin: (Sings, dances, collapses on couch.) To save yourself in a den of vipers bite first n' ask questions later, biting friend and enemy alike, for in a crises how is one to know the difference. (Snores.) The earth tongue laps the sky mouth—Eh? What? Play on, my French Ruski. Play! (He nods off. Felix stops; Yankee Doodle is low from above; Felix leans close to see if Rasputin is breathing. He wakes suddenly.) What!? You want to kiss me? You fuckin' dandy. Grr! Bring on the duchess!
Felix: (Picks up bottle.) Oo, you bark like a dog.
Rasputin: Fuck the same way, prissy piss ass. Bet you never dirty your hands.

Felix: Mais non. That's for jackasses, mon ami. Educate a jackass and he's no longer your jackass. God forbid I should have to stick my hands in dirt. The very idea is repulsive, makes me shudder. The bard was right: "I am made for better things." Only peasants dirty themselves, but they don't know any better. They're beasts of the field: coarse animals, dishonest, dirty and drunken; quarrel continually because they fear, suspect and despise each other. What filth, vermin, lower than the lowest. Who steals from his neighbors, sets fire to their property, bears false witness at court for a bottle of vodka? The peasant.

Rasputin: Yet some would say, they are human beings, suffer, weep, bleed like human beings. They have reasons, justifications. (Rattling on; disconnected; drowsy.) That they do. That they do! Grr! And something your privileged class doesn't know: crushing labor that makes the body ache at night, cruel winters, scanty crops, overcrowding, no help, and nowhere to look for help. They give their sweat and blood, and you give 'em the noose and the knout.

Felix: Have a sweet cake. You come from that stock, I believe. You know that life first-hand.

Rasputin: (Tosses bottle; rises, falls.) Where's my duchy-what-chee? Five minutes not a kopeck more, then I go to those crazy wandering souls, the gypsies—the salt of the earth. They make love with a knife. Cut you and kiss, drink your blood and eat your money; but by God, you come away knowing you've been kissed and fucked. Not like you nobles who fuck the people without the kiss. Ah! Where's my glass?

Felix: In your hand.

Rasputin: Which hand?

Felix: Left.

Rasputin: What's it doing there I'm right handed? (Tosses glass in fireplace.) Tfu! Now no hands! Another glass. (Felix obliges.) Fill it. Let it spill. When that duchess gets here, if she ever gets here, she'll lick it up, we'll pass it mouth to mouth. I lick it off her mountainous tits; suck it out of her aoul. (Spits.) Nas-dro-veeya! Where're you going?

Felix: To tell the Duchess of you're impatience.

Rasputin: I'm not patient. I'm pissed! Yes. Pissed! Tell her. No. You're right. What was that word? Im-pay, im-pay-shence. A much better word. I was born im-pay-shent. (Drinks.) One day the people will fall on your head like an avalanche. They'd be in their rights, too. Look at yourself. They don't have bread and you have palaces and wine cellars. You'd be lost without your canon fodder and all around jackasses.
Felix: God forbid that I should have to do my own laundry. Why I haven't wiped my own ass in years. Frankly, I've forgotten how.
Rasputin: Look out. Retribution's a bitch!
Felix: What keeps them from rising up, I wonder?
Rasputin: What holds back the ocean? Ignorant devotion, blind love. He is still Father Tsar, God's voice on earth.
Felix: And what drives you?
Rasputin: I gloat in destruction of evil.
Felix: Including your own?
Rasputin: Especially my own. Absolutely. Don't know why I have a talent for toppling deceit, a fondness really, for dispensing comeuppance.
Felix: That takes in the world.
Rasputin: A mother's work is never done. For now the royal court will suffice. HA! Tolstoy barefoot in farmer's clothes. Rediculous!
Felix: He wore a peasant's smock with balloon sleeves which is vogue these days among the young.
Rasputin: I was young when I came in here. The duchess is giving me the Yusupov two-step. Give me youth anytime because with it comes the balls to fuck every bitch and screw every lying bureaucrat and fawning diplomat. (Lifts glass.) Nasdrovia? (Drinks; pores another.) The poet's fancy, my dear, is like the church itself; seemingly in earnest, but utterly lost in circumstance. We are more Lucifer's children than God's. (Leaning in.) Stuck in a temporal body because should He grant immortality our arrogance would damn Him a fool. O, I'd love to be crucified.
Felix: I could arrange it.
Rasputin: What?
Felix: What're friends for, eh?
Rasputin: No nails. Nails hurt.
Felix: I should think.

Rasputin: Truss me up with holly hocks and vine leaves, a crown of juniper berries n' day lilies.
(MUSIC: cantata, sibilant, ominous with periodic silence.)
Rasputin: I'm no hypocrite. I cross myself before sinning and afterward, occasionally. Every blessed thing on earth is God's work. Birth, death, the seasons, the whole goddamn mess, it's all God's handiwork, His process of regeneration.
Felix: And you're the catalyst.
Rasputin: A cat-o-list with nine lives. Why me? Who knows? He made the boy a bleeder, my avenue to the aristocracy. Tfu! A misnomer if ever there was one. Fetch the Crutches. I mean, Duchess. (Felix exits.) Achtung, y'mongrel Cossacks! (Tosses bottle; Lights down, up on:)

Scene 6:
same as scene 4

Felix: O, that son-of-a-bitch!
Vasily: What?
Felix: He's breaking priceless vintages.
Boris: But did he eat the cakes?
Felix: A Veuve Clicquot. Pricless.
Pureshkevitch: The cakes, man. Did he eat?
Felix: Yes, yes. The bastard's an animal.
Vasily: My God! He must have the stomach of a goat.
Felix: A Veuve Clicquot, vintage 1863. Bang! Against the wall.
Pureshkevitch: You should've broken it on his head.
Felix: I came close. God! The best vintages wasted on a pig.
Pureshkevich: (Takes out a gun.) I'll go down and shoot him myself.
Boris: Hold off. It's quiet down there. Maybe he's dead.
Pureshkevich: Take it. Shoot him, or I will. Take it the gun, Felix.
Vasily: Who could ingest that much poison and live?
Boris: The devil. What's keeping him alive?
Felix: I tell you, my nerves are giving out.
Vasily: He coated his stomach. He's a suspicious bastard. He knows and he's playing along. Right now the police are surrounding the palace.
Pureshkevich: Get a grip, man. He drank, ate, and swallowed?
Felix: Enough to kill a horse.
Boris: (At door.) He's strong, you know.

Pureshkevich: Get back. You'll give us away. What was he doing when you left? Standing? Sitting?
Boris: What are we doing? That's the question.
Felix: The man's got powers, supernatural powers. I'd rather face a German canon. There's honor in that. Poison's coward's work.
Vasily: He drank? He swallowed? He's clever. Maybe he siphoned it off.
Felix: How? Up his nose follicles and out his cuticles?
Pureshkevich: Don't bandy words with him.
Vasily: The Tsarina knows. The police—
Pureshkevich: You're a broken record. Enough. Shoot him right off.
Felix: He didn't bathe. You believe it? Smells like a French whore.
Vasily: It turns women on.
Boris: How do you know that?
Vasily: Court gossip.
Pureshkevich: Vent the bastard with bullets.
Felix: God, I'm exhausted. He never blinks—the sign of a madman.
Pureshkevich: Go back. Shoot straight out. Don't wait. Do it, man! We'll come running. Whatever you do, don't shoot us. We're headed for the barn, let's not fiddle in the doorway.

Scene 7

(Same as scene 5; basement; enter Felix to find Rasputin gone.)

Felix: Grishka. (Pause; panicky.) Grishka!
Rasputin: (Looming up.) Boo! Ha! You're not the duchesss. Ahh! I go to the gypsies. Fortunetellers and dancing acrobats! They will steal your eyes, the gold from your teeth, and you love every minute.
Felix: That Christmas Tolstoy kissed father on both cheeks. Now I kiss you. Face the cross. Confess your sins. Only I stay and you go to hell.
Rasputin: Yes. Very likely. (Felix shoots.) O, my God! Betrayed. (Staggers, knocks over cross, falls, as others rush in.)
Pureshkevich: Is he dead? (Takes gun from a physically drained Felix.) Off the rug, swine, you soil it! (Kicks body.)
Boris: (By the stairs.) Thank God. It's done.
Vasily: Amen! (Goes to body, gingerly checks for pulse.)
Pureshkevich: What? Afraid of the dead?
Vasily: Nothing. No pulse. The beast is dead, praise God!
(Suddenly, Rasputin's eyes open; he grabs Vasily.)
Rasputin: Coward!
Vasily: Ahh! (Horrified.) What's it take? Shoot! Shoot!
(Boris retreats; the lights go out; reducing the room to candlelight.)
Rasputin: (In the shadows.) I'll tell the Tsarina everything.
Pureshkevich: How? From the grave!
Rasputin: If I die. Woe to Russia.

Pureshkevich: Woe to you! Joy to Russia! (Fires; Rasputin slithers out.)
Rasputin: (In the courtyard.) Cowards! I'll tell the Tsarina everything!
Pureshkevich: (Pursuing.) Tell her this! (Shoots, misses, fires, Rasputin drops in the snow; rushing up, wild eyed, circles, dances, kicks body.) Get up, dog of the devil! (Soldiers run in with others. Felix beats body with a steel press.)
Felix: Swine! Filthy dog! (He's pulled away.)
Boris: (Kicks the body.) Die! Despicable, vile, putrid scumbag!
Vasily: (Restraining him.) Enough.
Boris: What's enough with a devil? He might be alive yet!
Pureshkevich: (Moving L to R, jumping; ecstatic.) Do you see? Thy will is done! Grishka Rasputin, enemy of Russia, is dead! Rejoice! I, Vladimir Pureshkevich, have slain the monster. Hear me, God? O, Russia? Awake! Hear me! I, Vladimir Pureshkevich, have killed Grishka! Now you can breathe. If you are Russian, if you love your country, rejoice. Rejoice! Awake, sons of Russia! The enemy of Russia and the Tsar, Grishka Rasputin is dead! Glory be to God and heaven. I, Vladimir Pureshkevich, killed Grishka Rasputin, enemy of Russia and the Tsar!

MUSIC: hypnotic; serpentine rhythm in and out:)

Choir: God have mercy . . . (Repeat 5 times.)
When it's evening in the west
It's morning in the east
An Empire that never sleeps
On which the sun never sets . . . (Bells toll.)

Coachie: They wrapped the body in a blue curtain, drove to a bridge that crosses to the isle of Neva and dropped it in the freezing water. The body was still warm. They'd brought weights, but forgot to tie them to the body. These, together with Rasputin's fur coat and a snow boot, were thrown into the river. Back at the palace they found the other boot, the bloody rug, and burned them. Soon the news was all over Petrograd. Rasputin's boot was discovered washed up on the ice. Divers went down to fish him out. A post mortem revealed Rasputin had freed himself from the rope. His lungs were full of water which meant he wasn't dead when dumped in the river. His body lay at Chesme Chapel on the road outside Tsarkoe Selo. (Music low; plaintive waltz.) The Tsar hurried home from the front to comfort his wife. Significantly, to Kaiser Wilhelm the political fall out from Rasputin's death meant something more important to the German cause.

Cameo 3:

Chesme Chapel

(The Empress dressed in mourning enters; kneels at the coffin. The Tsar comes up to stand behind her.)

Scene 8

(St. Petersburg: kettle drums, guns thunder; fiery reds; flash scenes of frenzied Petrograd citizens carrying pitchforks, clubs, steel bars, guns and rifles, singly and in groups criss-crossing in revolutionary fervor at times greeting each other in solidarity, other times clashing in opposition. "Comrades!" "Bourgeois!" (Nasty.) Dazed individuals drift in and out. Church bells melt to a shrieking train whistle at the Zurich train station followed by waltz music on a PA system interrupted by: *All aboard! Zurich to Germania! Zurich-Allemande!*)

ACT THREE

Scene 1:
The Sealed Train
(Exiles Going Home.)

Time: March-April, 1917.
Place: Departure platform, Zurich station; train compartment; a corridor; Finland Station, St. Petersberg.
Characters: Coachie; Lenin; Grigorii Eseyevich Zinoviev; Nadya; Inessa; a score of émigrés; Fritz Platten, Swiss liaise; two German officers; General Ludendorf; President-Judge, played by Coachie; Sasha; Mrs. Ulyanov, played by Mamushka.

(Open dark with train whistle; scratchy waltz music on PA system broken by:)

PA: *All aboard! Zurich to Germania! Zurich-Allemande!*

(Lights up; bustling crowd of wartime travelers. Coachie turns from ticket window, weaves through crowd toward his carriage. Shrieking train whistle.)
(Indicating news headline at a kiosk.)

Coachie: War and now revolution. Nothing stops an idea whose time has come. Any second Russian exiles will burst onto this platform in a state joy n' anxiety, trailed by well-wishers n' naysayers.
(Train whistle.)

Conductor: *All aboard! Your carriage, sir, 19, midway.*
Coachie: Spacebo. Pardon, Madame. (With child eating cherries.) Such a beautiful child. How old? Five? You should be proud. Bet those cherries are sour. No? Adieu, Madame. (Lowered voice.) Did you see, in the center of the dish there was a heart with a double-headed eagle Imperial Crest of Russia. The swirling juice made the heart look like it was bleeding.
(Train whistle.)
PA: *All aboard! Zurich to Germania! Zurich-Allemande!*
Coachie: The Tsar failed to read the will of the people. He thought they'd always love him no matter what, and for good reason. When speaking his name people crossed themselves twice, fell on their knees, proclaimed undying faith to his every utterance no matter how stupid. To the people, the Emperor was God on earth. In a vague sort of way Tsar Nicholas believed it himself. He read the people's mood by putting his finger on his own pulse, which beat in three-quarter time. In 1905 the Cossacks made a big mistake. They shot into a crowd of peaceful marchers and petitioners led by Father Gapon killing unarmed men, women, and children. It marked the beginning of the end of blind adoration. Frankly, had it not been for the war the revolution would've happened sooner maybe 1914, 1915 at the latest. In 1917 there was wide spread discontent with a calloused and intolerable autocracy, poverty, starvation, lack of military supplies resulting in needless mounting military deaths in a war nobody wanted. What touched it off? A Petrograd mother got mad. You won't find her name in a book. Tfu! Nyet! Let me explain in case you never had a mother. Mess with mama you get the rolling pin and more than you bargained for. Ha! Lenin himself said there could never be revolution without the women. A mother standing on a bread line all night with starving children in sub zero weather, and the baker slams the door in her face. "No bread! Quota filled. Come back tomorrow!" Tfu! That was the revolution in a nutshell: one holier than thou, blazing angry mother with mouths to feed. She goes, *tomorrow? Tfu! My children will be dead. Give me bread now!* She throws a rock through his window, other mothers join in screaming, *Give us bread!* This time the Cossacks refused to shoot women and children. The men streamed out of the factories and together they

ransacked bakeries, granaries, and looted the rich. The question for Lenin in Zurich was, *how to get home to join the revolt before it faded.* Some said, *Through France!* Others said, *England to Sweden. They're Russia's allies.* Lenin goes, *but not ours, a bunch of "crazy" revolutionaries. They might detain us for weeks checking passports. No. The quickest way is a straight line through Germany.* It's also the quickest way to get shot.

(A group bursts onto the platform, pushes through the crowd.)

Coachie: Now it starts. The short, almond-eyed one with red hair and beard is Lenin, the idea whose time has come. To his right is Grigorii Zinoviev, one of his oldest and closest collaborators, on his left is the Swiss socialist Fritz Platten, liaise traveling with them.

(As they go by.)

Voices: Home at last! Is it real or a hoax?

Zinoviev: Who can say? Could be a setup and we'll all be shot.

Voices: Germany? It's not crazy, it's nuts! If they shoot you the party's done! They won't honor the pact.

Fritz: Move aside, please.

Coachie: *Lenin worked a deal with the Germans: two private "sealed" carriages, travel permits, and under the table a satchel of deutschemarks on a promise to pull out of the war. Later, Winston Churchill characterized the affair, saying, "What the Germans did is the equivalent of unleashing bacilli on the Russian people." Tfu! (Shrieking train whistle.)*

PA: All aboard! Zurich-Allemande! All aboard!

Coachie: (Climbs aboard.) They call it Lenin's Sealed Train.

Anon Voices: Sealed trap, if y'ask me. Nobody's askin'. You'll get your keisters shot! Russia or the grave, never in-between.

Coachie: Nobody likes to admit that in a crisis they caved in to fear, embraced the enemy, or the abhorrent and unthinkable to become the thing they most dreaded.

Anon Voices: Your health, comrades. (Drinks from flask.) And to you. Nasdrovia! Economic determinism's the answer. Kiss the Kaiser for us! Don't bother writing. We'll read about you in the obituaries.

Travelers Man and wife: Who are those people? Bolsheviks. They look like funeral directors going to a pallbearer's convention. Where is our car, dear? Further down. The further, the better.
Voices: How we make a living determines how we live, our actions, what sort of government rules. Bankers, industrialists, shopkeepers, under capitalism each group rips off the other. There's a new day happening in Russia. Out with the old rotters. Au revoir. I'd drink to that but I'm fresh out. Cause you drink to anything. Take a swig of mine. Nasdrovia!
(From a train compartment doorway to a well-wisher.)
Nadya: We'll send news! Yes. Yes. Adieu! Adieu!
Anon: Bon voyage! Where's Ilych?
Nadya: There, there he is. This way, Ilych! Over here! Quick!
Conductor: All aboard! (Train whistle.)
Nadya: Ilych, this way!
(Lenin, Zinoviev are buffeted about as they push through.)
Lenin: I hate this God-awful mess! Move, idiot! (Shoves someone.)
Zealot: It's a Fritzie trick!
Zinoviev: Make way!
Lenin: Move aside! (Cat calls.)
Zealot: You can't go.
Lenin: I can and I will. Get your filthy hands off me! (Pulls gun.) Back off!
Zealot Voices: Traitors! Saboteurs!
Lenin: Myopic fools!
Zealot: Colluding with the enemy! We're at war with Germany!
Lenin: Thank you for that piece of news, comrade. But beyond your nose there's a bigger picture. Take your head out of your navel! Look beyond your neighbor, and the rotting villages of your country! Why are you in exile? For the just life not only at home but in the whole world.
Anon: You'll be shot on the way, comrade!
Lenin: We have assurances!
Anon: The Kaiser assured the Tsar. A million dead Russians prove it.
Lenin: Revolutions wait for no man.
Anon: What's another day?

Lenin: Every day is critical. Right now the Tsar's power is slowly being taken over by the capitalist bourgeoisie.
Mixed Voices: Give 'em hell! Bon voyage! Traitors! Patriots! Screw you! (Someone pushes up.) I just heard from my uncle in Petersburg. He says, it's unbelieveable, a dream. People're talking openly for the first time. They walk wherever they want. If a door is closed they break it down. But there are factions and one has to be alert or get shot. Looting, burning, breaking into homes of the rich, drinking wine. It's magnificent.
Anonymous Voices: Bon voyage! Adieu! Au revoir!
Lenin: Let me pass. Spacebo. Pardonez moi. Phone your uncle, say, help is on the way.
Nadya: (From a carriage away.) Here! Over here!
Zinoviev: There's Nadya, (Waves back.) midway. Come.
Lenin: I'm right. They're wrong. To hang back now? Tfu!
(They scramble into the compartment; others find open doors and get aboard.)

Scene 2

(General greetings; hugs, kisses.)

Lenin: Not to strike while the iron is hot—

Nadya: What's he mumbling?

Zinoviev: Skeptics, detractors.

Lenin: Idiots! Afraid of their own shadows. (At window.) Hang back and the whole thing could pass us by.

Nadya: Let's settle down. We've a long trip ahead.

Lenin: This is the right move.

Nadya: Absolutely.

Zealot: (Apace with moving train.) In Germania kiss your ass goodbye!

Lenin: Every stripe of idiocy. I expected no less. Read about us on the tableaux d'affiche down at the lake! We must be bold. Is everyone here?

Nadya: All but Inessa. She had unfinished business.

Lenin: Business? What business? There is only this business, this train.

(Nadya shrugs.)

Inessa: (Suddenly in doorway.) Perdonez moi, but is this compartment free? It appears full of dangerous revolutionaries. O, but beggars can't be choosie. It was close, but here I am with minutes to spare. (Train jolts forward; falls into Lenin's arms.) Oops! The shortest distance between two points is a train jolt. Pardonez moi, monsieur.

Lenin: Il n'ya pas rien, m'dame. As I was saying, never let fear ruin an opportunity. What will happen to us? Who knows? One thing is certain; in Switserland one is completely out of touch, dead to himself and the world. Another week there and you could can stick me in a clock and on the hour I'll come out, go, cuckoo, cuckoo, and blow my brains out.

All: (Laughter.) Cuckoo! Cuckoo! Bong! Boing!)

Lenin: Look at those monkeys out there? It's no secret what we do!

Zinoviev: It better be to the German foot soldier. The last thing we need's a gun happy Fritzie.

Lenin: We have German liaise, the car has extra-territorial privileges.

Zinoviev: A game of footsie with the devil.

Lenin: Free passage in exchange for German-Austrian prisoners held in Russia, and a promise to end a war which we've never been for anyway.

Zinoviev: I hope the people at home see it your way.

Lenin: Nothing is certain in this world, Grigorii. You could walk down the street and get hit by a falling brick. We take a lot of things on faith. The question is, will the future greet us with open arms?

Zinoviev: We telegraphed Milyukov, but never heard back.

Lenin: What can you expect from a scoundrel?

Zinoviev: Maybe they'll shoot us on arrival.

Lenin: Me? They'll hang. O, my head.

Nadya: Your pills, Ilya.

Lenin: Yes, yes. (Pops some pills.)

Zinoviev: Where are the sandwiches?

Inessa: I feel like playing the piano. Anyone remember to bring a piano. O, I have one in my bag. (Rolls out a make believe keyboard, plays and hums a waltz.) Da, da, da-da, da-dum.

Nadya: (Leaning back.) O, my. My feet haven't touched earth in days.

Lenin: In thirty minutes gather everyone in the corridor. Have Fritz brief them on rules and then I'll talk. (Inessa hums, rises, and waltzes about.)

Nadya: Inessa, I doubt you ever heard the words *sit still*. I was just thinking of Bronski's description of the look on your face, Ilych, when he gave you the news. You were fixing the break pads on your bicycle and go, "Da, da," followed by an expression that said, and the moon is made of green cheese. He had to drag you down to the lake. O, yes. Reading the news you began howling, jumping like a ten year old. Then suddenly pensive, you go, "Bronski, maybe it's a rouse?"

Lenin: Laugh, but the news is scanty. Who is in charge? Has the Tsar abdicated? Is he forming a counter revolution? Chances are Guchkov, Milyakov, and those mongrel Menshevik conciliators are consorting with the bourgeois imperialists forming a defencist government. Well, we shall see about that. When a miracle drops in your lap, even half of one, only a fool ignores it. The World War has been a regisseur to revolution in Russia and soon the world. We must give thanks for their suicidal ignorance. Ha! We are like those crazy American buckaroo cowboys who chase steers with lassos, galloping along on a steel horse, ready to rope the future, wrestle it to the ground, and brand it.

Zinoviev: I give you my feint, yippee.

Inessa: What brand? RU, Rancho Utopia.

Lenin: According to my crystal ball—

Nadya: We didn't pack one.

Zinoviev: He means the pate atop his forehead.

Lenin: "On s'engage et puis, on voit."

(Lights up in corridor; group singing Stenka Razin, or the International.)

Fritz: Despite difficult bargaining with the Germans in Berne, we're underway.

Voice: In which direction? Heaven or hell! (Laughter.)

Fritz: I remind you of the ground rules. Verstehen?

Voices: Vistach! Speak Russian. From now on only Russian! (Cheers.)

Fritz: No crossing the chalk line. Your coach is sealed off at both ends. I'll be forward in the German compartment. All questions should be addressed to me. I shall take them up with the Germans. Lastly, no contact outside the group whatsoever. We petitioned Swedish authorities for travel permits. They know our route, that we're underway, and how to reach us. We should get word before Berlin.

Voices: (Among themselves.) Screw Sweden. I'll ski home. (Cheers.) If they refuse us passage, which is possible, we'll lose several days backing up and going around them.
Voice: A nice fix. (Lenin steps into corridor.)
Voice: What about Sweden?
Lenin: Good skiing, I'm told. We'll go around them. Eh? That's exactly what we'll do if we must. No wavering, comrades. One way or another we're going home. I vow it. (Cheers.) Grigorii, come away from the window. You might accidentally fall out, or were you thinking to save yourself by jumping while there is still time? (Laughter.) Let us hope we never wish we had. (Cheers.) Many good comrades wrongly chided us for what we are doing. They meant well. "Too soon," they cried. But I say, "If not now, when?" Wait for a more auspicious time? Have we not been waiting for years? In monotonous Switzerland each day was like the day before. I had to smack myself in the face to keep from falling asleep. The Swiss are good people. But politically, the only valid Swiss Movement is in their cuckoo clock. No, my friends. We, the avant guard of international socialism, entertain no thoughts of hanging back in the face of opportunity. Revolutions wait for no man. Carpe diem! Our moment has come. Carpe diem! Seize the day! (Cheers.) Revolutions have a will and duration of their own. Right now the people are leaderless. Doubtless there is a temporary government of sorts, a backwash of the old, corrupt and scummy monarchy—usurers, and bureaucratic yes-men. So, it is imperative that we get home as soon as possible. Lastly, and this needs repeating, bring your problems to Fritz who will broach them to the German officers. Also, absolutely no fraternizing outside our group. (Voice: But if she's a beautiful frauline?) Bring her to me first. My advice is keep your mouth and your fly buttoned up. Just think of the good Russian women waiting in Petersburg—(Voices: Who? Your mother.) One slip risks everything. Even with extraterritorial rights, who knows? We might encounter doubters and provocateurs, hotheads and fools who need little excuse to shoot a bunch of long standing *dangerous Russian revolutionaries.* (Voices: Who? Us? No.) Stay close and keep to yourselves. C'est ça? One last essential point. In Berne Fritz Platten worked out an agreement, which I accepted.

We gave up little in return. They want us to pull out of the war. It's no secret. We've never been pro-War. We promised to do our best and they bought it. They want us out of the war so they can concentrate their forces in the west. Good. Let them kill each other for all the good they do humanity. To them, we're "crazy Russian sectarians." (Voice: True!) Our obligation is to agitate and propagandize for socialism. What is that, something new? Comrades, this train ride is the first step toward socialism. According to Liebnecht and Luxemburg, our socialist contacts in Germany, the people there are also anti-war, and on the cusp of civil war. Capitalism is doomed, foisted on its own petard about to devour itself out of avarice and incurable greed. We are the torchbearers of worldwide socialism. When Prussian royalist generals become psychologists there is something in it for us Russian revolutionaries. Imagine! We are entering the first stage of the first people's revolution, which will neither be final or limited to Russia. Our first task is propagandizing for an international proletarian revolt, and for conquest of power in Russia by the Soviets of Workers' Deputies. Our words must not be abstractions, but grasped easily by the people. (Voice: Bread! Land! Peace!) Exactly. History tells us revolutions take fire. We must not stand on principle if it jeopardizes the cause. We, the avant guard cadre of an international proletariat, are going to fan the flames already started. Burn out the warmongers! Torch a decadent, vicious nobility! Our imperative: "Assume leadership." To hell with Milyukov, Kerensky, Guchkov, and their temporary government! It's the old European pattern revived not to bring peace, but to destroy the revolution, and chain the people all over again. I say, No! No! No! Our first priority is to quit the war and build a socialist state. Some think not, that we made a pact with the West. Tfu! Who are Russia's allies anyway? Do they have a special love for Russia? To the West we are a balance of power, merely a tool for détente. The British and French are ready to fight to the last Russian. What does the Tsar think, or his Hessian wife? She strikes me as one infused with traditions and nuances of Russian medievalism, the most meager and crude of all medievalism, at a time when the people are striving to free themselves from bondage. This so-called Tsarina, the Nemka!—This princess, this hemophilia carrier, is literally possessed by the demon of autocracy, having come from her rural corner to the heights of Byzantine despotism to rule an empire alien to her and her maniac confidant Rasputiin. Now, for the moment, rest yourselves, conserve water and food, and dream the impossible has happened, that several days hence, after years of waiting and longing, and suffering, this emigrant train shall pull into Finland Station in Petersburg, and you, comrades, shall plant your weary feet on the terra firma of your motherland. (Cheers. In compartment.)

Zinoviev: We'd better write ahead.

Lenin: Have Fritz check for home news at the next stop. Toward what end is the revolution going? I can't put down substantial ideas without facts. Has the temporary government entered an agreement with the Tsar? Is he still in power, or not? Is he preparing a counter-revolution? Our immediate task is to broaden the scope of our work: organize the masses, arouse new social strata among the backward elements of the rural population, and domestic servants, to form nuclei in the military for the purpose of carrying on a detailed exposé of government to prepare for total seizure of power by Soviet Workers' Deputies. Only an armed proletariat can bring peace. When the present government says it wants peace it means business as usual, and a piece of you to get it. The real danger is counter-revolution, resistance from monarchists who will organize a party and perhaps an army to regain their losses. If the Tsar should escape or gain support of part of the army it's possible that in order to deceive the people he will issue a manifesto on the subject of an immediate peace, which he will sign with Germany. We must show them merciless resistance, and *crush the tsarist monarchy completely*. Hereditary rights or positions of rule are mal-a-propos gains and therefore intolerable. History shows us time and again where that road leads us only too well. The day of primogenitor has gone the way of dinosaurs. We bought that ludicrous hogwash long enough. Leadership will no longer come from the top, but from below, from various soviet workers' deputies. The people have seen the light and rebelled. Now it is up to us to awaken in each man that inner priest or internal truth which is every man's innate sense of right and wrong. No more petty squires and philistines! Out with them;

lock; stock; and barrel. Let's not fool ourselves. What I say will not be easy. There will be resistance as in Plato's cave parable. The light will blind them, but they will come round to seeing right from wrong. It's inbred and avoidable. The demands of thought and the answers are an ageless struggle between theory and practicality. It is not enough that thought should seek to realize itself; reality must also strive toward thought. We can never sustain leadership with fancy polemics and big words. We must speak to the people in simple words found in meaningful slogans directly recognizable like comic book pictures. We don't want people's admiration only their cooperation. To earn their respect we must speak in words easily understand. If we get high-minded and they start scratching their heads wondering what we meant, we lose them. We the more fortunate ones have a duty to raise the conscience of the less endowed, to reawaken their beaten down self-respect, to sustain their natural born sense of justice, to encourage them to stand up unafraid to demand a fair share of what they produce and insist on their rights as human beings. In the words of Victor Hugo: *There is one thing stronger than all the armies in the world, and that's an idea whose time has come.* When people are willing to die for their beliefs they are unstoppable.

Zinoviev: I like "Power to the people!" Bread and Land is good.

Lenin: Yes. Make a note. (Pensive.) At about this time we'd be down at the lake for the latest postings, living off scraps of news—

Zinoviev: Drips and drabs and praying for this day.

Lenin: Impossible to separate fact from fiction.

Nadya: Chiedze's speech was clear enough.

Lenin: The ultimate compromise, and from a Menshivik. Well, the leopard doesn't change its spots.

Nadya: After we get home there'll be a new kind of posting at the lake.

Lenin: I confess I was not so bold as to burn our bridges completely, I left some money behind in case. Imagine if we stayed behind issuing directives from Zurich? (Mockingly) Our tactical approach is: No trust in or support of the provisional committee! Don't trust Kerensky! No rapprochement with other parties!

Zinoviev: We should get up a few directives now.

Lenin: "On s'engage et puis, on voit." First, you commit, and then you see. One thing is certain. We must destroy the phony government lock, stock, and barrel! They're rigmarole defencist policy is to go on duping the people in the name of duty and country, filling their own plate while the masses starve.
Inessa: Once your foot is in the door, then what? Old habits die-hard.
Lenin: First we'll allow for capitalist thinking in business until the people are educated about production. The second stage is the transitional one, using capitalist methods to take over and learn the means of production. The third stage of complete socialism will happen when the people are fully educated in how to maintain and run the factories, and mines, etc. Then we establish a Republic of Soviets, Workers, and Peasants to control production and distribute goods. Nationalize all banks under Soviet control; confiscate all private lands. There must be a rebuilding of the revolution and the destruction of the bourgeois state establishment—army, police, bureaucracy—to be replaced by Soviet organizations made up of officials elected by the people and replaceable at any time. Rule from below not from above!
Zinoviev: A dictatorship of the proletariat.
Lenin: Yes. We must explain to the masses, especially to the proletariat and frontline troops, how they were misled. One immediate task is to encourage fraternization with German troops.
Nadya: The people have done the impossible. They must be drunk with enthusiasm.
Lenin: Lots of people have died for this moment. We shall not disappoint them. Who could've imagined it?
Nadya: You. You ate, drank and slept it.
Inessa: Now you play Faust to the devil.
Lenin: Not quite. I indulged in their wishful thinking. They bought conjecture. I bought immediacy. It remains to be seen who comes out ahead. What we anticipate seldom happens; what we least expect generally does.
Nadya: Ilych, you're a long distance runner with great determination.
Lenin: Time will tell.

Nadya: The only person who has more illusions than the dreamer is the man of action.
Lenin: What did we give up, really? We both want Russia out of the war but for different reasons. They deceive themselves if they think we're allies. For the moment we're convenient footstools for one another. Theirs will be kicked out from under them by civil war. Among bankers there is a maxim: In any deal there is always a fool. Look around. If you can't find him it's you.

(Lights down, up on Lenin and Nadya at chess. Lenin's haunt is Sasha death, a periodic loop varying from visual to strictly audio.)

Judge: You leave the court no recourse.
Sasha: You leave the people less.
Judge: A puppy. Hardly seen life.
Sasha: Yet what I've seen is detestable.
(Gaveling; drum roll; gallows in silhouette.)
Sasha: Marx was right. Under capitalism labor is alienation, external to the worker's essential self. In his work he denies himself, is discontented, and destroys his mind. The worker is only at home when not at work. As soon as no physical or other compulsion exists such labor is shunned like the plague. Work in which man alienates himself is labor of self-sacrifice, of mortification, and results in the horrible loss of himself as a unique human being. He becomes a stranger to himself without a moral compass. It's everyman's duty to free himself from petty squires and philistines who use and abuse workers for egoistic ends. (Gaveling.) What can I say, so long, love you, embrace, and kiss? There is only time to die with dignity. I am that part of you which believes in fairness and truth, prefers tact over confrontation, that part born in you that intuitively understands right from wrong. I enjoy making things out of wood, playing chess, but above all I love truth. Something about truth and honesty always touched a sympathetic chord in me. I detest lies and usury, and yet government officials display an aversion to truth, to human language, to cries for decency, and respect for individuality. I love natural history, philosophy, languages, and words. Like—

Lenin and Sasha: Butterfly nets, test tubes. Leaves pressed between pages; jars of specimen from the Sviaga River. Remember? We'd swim and fish in the meandering Sviaga. When boring relatives came calling, we'd say, Oblige us with your absence! Whole summers—No work and all play. Oblige us with your absence! Remember Kouskino, the white house with the columns, steamer up the Volga to Kazan, the carriage ride to the summer house, everyone crammed in tight among suitcases and wicker hampers? Whole summers, no work, all play; endless days merged one into the other. Ou e le niege d'hier? Mushrooms frying in sour cream. (Gaveling.) Look, Sash, my pencil, sharp as a stiletto. (Echoey.) Ha, ha! Country gentlemen! Two mushrooms frying in sour cream. Ha, ha! Two mushrooms frying in sour cream.

(Shrieking train whistles; Berlin siding, Potsdam, Lenin and Ludendorf.)

Ludendorf: Bratwurst from Potsdam, Heir Lenin. We'll continue to funnel expenses to you inside Russia through Parvus' Finland based trading company. Good luck on your journey. In the package is very gudt sauerkraut undt mustard. Yah. My aid will bring more before—how shall I put it?—continuing your *mission*. Auf widersein. (Lenin goes.)

Aide: Let's shoot them all.

Ludendorf: In good time.

Aid: A few dead Russians more or less—

Ludendorf: Sabotage, Herr Loitner, is an effective demoralizer. Don't you agree? It makes for rot within. We mustn't be rash in underestimating those ragamuffins. They will do our dirty work because they've no choice. Should they gain control, succeed in undermining Russian resolve—

Aide: Weaken the army and the monarchy—

Ludendorf: Correct. Then we walk right in, Herr Loitner. What a fool does in the end, a wise man does in the beginning. (Fade out.)

Scene 3: (same as Scene 2)

Nadya: Would you rather rest? (Lenin moves a chess piece.) We've been bouncing about and off each other for years, hoping and praying for this moment. Maybe it ends now. (She moves a piece; He counters.) Look out for what you want you're liable to get it.

Zinoviev: Get what, who can say?

Lenin: We shall find out soon enough. Fortunately, it comes while we still have strength in our muscles and legs to carry us.

Nadya: How far we've come, Ilych, since Siberia. Ages ago. We've grown older but our views remain the same.

Lenin: I think around the edges we were starting to become desperate.

Nadya: Weary, I should think. We're less impulsive, more patient, I'd say. Ha. I first saw you one Christmas at a rally in the school stadium,

Lenin: No. It was at a party.

Nadya: When we met, yes. But my first sight of you was at a sports game twenty-five years ago. You were sitting several rows below in the stands. I knew right away. I pointed you out to my girlfriend. She said, *that little fellow with red hair and almond eyes? O, I know him from the school paper. Always serious with a book in his hand. I don't know.* I go, *What?* She says, *He only has one suit.*

Lenin And I'm still wearing it. (Moves piece.) Who needs more traps?

Nadya: I was shy and hadn't the courage to speak up. I asked her to introduce us. She went to you, said a few words, turned to call me; but I had run off to the lady's room, nauseous, and threw up.

Later, she introduced us at a party. And we've been "partying" ever since pardon the pun.
Lenin: (Chuckling.) It was a church social.
Zinoviev: Now that's irony.
Nadya: A Shrovetide party in Petrograd, spring of '93. Don't ask what we were doing there.
Lenin: Free food.
Nadya: Certainly not Shriving, an act of penance.
Zinoviev: What's it mean?
Nadya: Shrovetide is three days before Ash Wednesday, the time for confession before Lent. Shrove Sunday, Monday and Tuesday. A time for confession, absolution, to be shriven before dying. Years later we met on vacation and married in July, 1898 in the Siberian village Shushenskoye. I was exiled to Ufa and had to marry quickly to stay with Ilych, but his identification papers hadn't reached the district superintendent.
Lenin: Bureaucracy even in Siberia! I was already in my second year of exile!
Nadya: Yet without that document we couldn't marry.
Lenin: The district police superintendent says, (Sternly) *I know nothing about you. I can't issue a marriage certificate. Tfu!* Finally, a local cleric conducted the ceremony.
Lenin: My dog Shu-shu was best man. Good old Shu-shu. Probably gone now. A dog lives what, fifteen years? A wonderful companion on bleak days and cold nights. We hunted together and went fishing together when the snow and ice melted. Your friend, what was her name? Apolinara, the minx.
Nadya: She was a sweet woman. The party was a church social and fundraiser.
Lenin: With infantile religious brain washing. Free food. Enticements for starving youth, and punch laced with vodka from private stock. The talk hasn't changed since: student rights, freedom of the press, Russia's future. A young fellow, I recall, said, *What Russia needs are literacy committees to educate the masse.* I still laugh to this day. *Well,* I said, *anybody who wants to save the Fatherland with literacy committees, why fine. We shall say go ahead, and do our best not to interfere.* The young man had a point. I prefer stronger methods.

Nadya: Nothing has changed since then including your suit.
Lenin: The cabbage soup is thinner.
Nadya: Back then my tiresome stomach trouble hardly mattered, or so it seems now. Then a letter would arrive, O, did we splurge and feast. Butter for the bread, an onion for the soup.
Lenin: In 1895 in Petrograd we were involved in illegal political activities; wrote leaflets for underground workers' circles, organized strikes. My brother's reputation preceded me. You were less suspect and more easily the breadwinner. You clerked somewhere—
Nadya: In the railway administration. Nights I taught Marxism to factory hands, discussed proletarian conditions. Here and there I'd slip in some socialism.
Lenin: The Tsarist police, those insidious watchdogs, kept an eye on me. Speaking freely was dangerous. I never knew who in an audience or among my associates might be an undercover agent. In public forums I urged people to listen beyond the words, to what was behind them. I had always to be careful to leave out specific names, and words like Tsar and monarchy. I spoke instead about new laws that favored employers, of Cabinet Ministers who were anti-working class. To speak openly of the Tsar could alienate certain audiences—
Nadya: Workers and peasants.
Lenin: To them, the Tsar was still sacrosanct, their Little Father. So I alluded mostly to his ministers. They were the culprits. Of course, they were all in it together.
Nadya: But we found subtle ways of reminding them of their birthright.
Lenin: Educating the people on the one hand while on the other eluding the police at every turn, slipping out of the 'detectives' net. Ha. Good Narodnaya Volya training. Eventually, they got me. In prison I wasted no time. I used their library; received books sent by family, food parcels and money for bribes. My health then was satisfactory. I drank mineral water brought to me from the pharmacy. I exercised, slept 9 hours a day, and dreamt about the various chapters of my future books. I can still do 50 pushups in quick succession without bending my knees. The guard peeping into my cell must've thought I'd grown pious suddenly though I

never once asked to visit the prison church. Maybe once or twice to get out of the cell. Nights I read fiction to relax. I talked regularly with cell neighbors using a secret code of knocks for letters of the alphabet. We even played chess by the knock code. Part of me regretted getting released early. It's true. A little longer I would've finished my book. One day I received a pile of letters from every corner of Russia. Letters always put me in a holiday mood. Then I landed in Shushenskoye, christened Shu-shu-shu—Not a bad place. I rented a room in a peasant's hut; and had complete liberty of movement. I'd write home: send me your newspaper after you've read it; send my kid gloves. I wanted them in the summer to protect against mosquitoes. You can put a net over your head, but the hands are always attacked. One day I returned from hunting and saw a light in my hut. The peasant owner told me Oskar Alesandrovich a Petrograd worker in exile was in there drunk and throwing my books around. I ran in—

Nadya: And I leaped on you from behind the door. Surprise! We talked for a long time that night.

Zinoviev: I'll bet.

Lenin: For the most part we could travel in the province, hold jobs, and if you had money even marry; but most importantly Siberia was a training ground for revolutionaries in exile. The first thing I discovered was that sometimes a person met once and never again can influence us more than some we've known for years. Life moves in strange ways. You can live around the corner from someone who'll play an important role in your life years later; and yet, while you live a block from each other you are strangers. When I was expelled from Kazan University there was at that time a fellow named Nikolai Fedoseev living in Kazan, but we never met until ten years later on a train to Siberia. The man had compiled a catalogue; or reading list for social democrats that was *the* best reference book anyone had ever put together. He was of enormous help guiding me through political literature and opening the way to Marxism. I wrote Plekhanov plans and schemes with fellow Marxists, even completed one of my earliest efforts: *The Development of Capitalism In Russia.*

Inessa: Life wherever you are presents choices.

Lenin: Bloody few in Siberia. Sink or swim. That which doesn't kill you makes you stronger. I had books, pencils, no ink, it would freeze! I read and wrote, and Shu-shu under the table kept my feet warm.
Nadya: Peat for a fire. Hang over it a pot of snow. When it melts toss in tealeaves and you're set for the day sipping and writing. The air filled with the fragrance of mint. Mm!
Lenin: I could go for some tea now. Our bodies fly through Germany, but our thoughts are already in Petrograd. Soon one will catch up with the other. Sink or swim. So many thoughts, feelings, tumbling about. There is justice in life.
Zinoviev: Damn little. We're not out of the woods yet.
Lenin: This old suit of mine, wrinkled and frayed, how does it look?
Nadya: Wrinkled and frayed. (Chuckling.)
Lenin: Is it presentable?
Nadya: What's the choice? It or nothing.
Inessa: Nothing would be impressive.
Nadya: Hang your jacket. It'll straighten the wrinkles.
Lenin: Have the Swiss ever produced anything but clocks?
Zinoviev: Swiss cheese.
Inessa: The Vatican guards. No wars.
Zinoviev: It's the mountains and the snow. It'd take years to dig them out, and then what would you have?
All: Clocks and Swiss cheese.
Lenin: Rome never imagined an army advancing over the Alps.
Nadya: With elephants no less.
Lenin: Soon we'll be descending on Petersburg. The Provisional Government will look up and find we're the elephant in the room.
Nadya: Ilych, I want to abolish competition. It vulgarizes the soul. People have it in their noggins that competition is the measure of man.
Zinoviev: We'll all be measured soon enough.
Lenin: It's the fault of government.
Zinoviev: Please. We're born to compete. As soon as we can walk we push each other around. Who's King of the hill? It's the animal in us.

Lenin: And that animal has become the monster capitalism.
Inessa: Can two people have identical dreams?
Zinoviev: They'd need the same brain. Hopes and aspirations can be similar if linked to a common desire.
Nadya: I'll settle for two people on the same page.
Inessa: Desire and dreams bring the unexpected. What's life without surprise? A life like a government should be in flux, a state of constant revolution always evolving and devolving. Revolution, evolution, and revelation.
Lenin: Someone is selling my medicine. Our Alps is gaining the confidence of people.
Inessa: O, je m'excuse! I almost forgot. Rosa Luxemberg is quoted in the German socialist news. Let me see. E voila.
Lenin: You read it. Give us a synopsis, the gist of it.
Nadya: Is the movement making headway?
Inessa: *She calls the Russian revolution the mightiest event of our time . . . It was, still is, the clearest condemnation of the lying establishment, of the lying phrases which government zealously supplied at the start of WW I as an ideological cover for German imperialism's campaign of conquest . . .* She went on to say . . . *it is evidence of the people's anger at what leadership has done with the trust given to them by the people—*
All: Here! Here!
Inessa: Furthermore, she says, *It signals that the people are not fools, that they have a long memory, and sooner or later they will rise up and demand—*
Lenin: Their pound of flesh.
Inessa: Yes. *The piper be paid.* She said, *now I see the real meaning of revolution. It stands for the people's right to overthrow a corrupt government anytime, anyplace, anyhow.*
Lenin: Good, good. Thank you.
Inessa: O, she also said, *Politicians easily forget their sworn obligation to the people to always do right by them, and the severe consequences of doing wrong.*
Lenin: Witness the French revolution. We must avoid their fate. We don't want to eat our own.
Zinoviev: We should send word ahead. (Inessa looks at Lenin.)

Lenin: I can't commit without details. Distance puts one at a disadvantage.

Zinoviev: I'll work up a generic in my compartment. I'll say, underway, our numbers, time of arrival.

Lenin: Give a rough quote Rosa attributed to the Socialist news release.

Zinoviev: I'll bring it to you in ten minutes.

Lenin: Take your time. It's a long trip.

Zinoviev: Nadya, will you help?

Nadya: Yes, of course. Give me five minutes to powder my nose. (She and Zinoviev exit.)

Inessa: Distance puts one at a disadvantage.

Lenin: So does a cluttered playing field.

(They embrace; shrieking train whistle; strobe light effect as train hurtles in and out of tunnels.)

Together: Danger! Animal Crossing! Falling Rocks! Bury me deep. Deep! More coal, Mr. Engineer! The stoker fires the engine. He can't see round the bend. He relies on trust. On s'engage et puis, on voit.

Lenin: I confess I had doubts.

Inessa: It was inevitable.

Lenin: I doubted this moment, doubted this day would come in my lifetime.

Inessa: Love and revolution, the elemental flux of life. (Shrieking train whistle.)

Together: Bury me deep, Mr. Engineer! I could eat you with a spoon.

Lenin: I dread stepping from the train. Will I be shoulder-to-shoulder with you or escorted to Peter and Paul?

Inessa: Take me in your arms! Devour me. I'm yours.

Lenin: Tonight while you sleep they burn the midnight oil—

Inessa: I died a hundred times over getting here.

Lenin: Scheming how to regain what you have rightfully taken.

Inessa: In the cab my heart bursting, I ran all the way holding the wind chimes.

Lenin: Their greedy paws are already in your pocket.

Together: Animal Crossing! Landslide! Keep vigil. Deep. Deeper! Shovel that coal, Mr. Engineer! This is a glorious day! Life in flux.

(Shrieking train whistle.)
Lenin: Here, now, we say to the whore mongering capitalists—
Lenin-Inessa: Imperial-autocratic dogs! Decadent bourgeoisie! Business as usual is over! Bread! Land! Peace! Like it? Love it.
Lenin: How can theory encompass adequately the indiscernible, protean, and elusive substance of collective intercourse? Principles accepted in theory but disregarded in practice.
Inessa: An Olympian Schemata.
Lenin: Allegiance to principles has hamstrung many socialists.
Inessa: Not you.
Lenin: We must appeal to primordial desires—
Inessa: The inarticulate peasant.
Lenin: Love is a mélange of ratiocination—
Inessa: Pragmatism.
Lenin: Trust and deceit.
Inessa: The age old—
Lenin: Elemental flux. Fire bred in the bone.
Inessa: We fluxing or flapping?
(Shrieking train whistle.)
Inessa: I brought you wind chimes.
Lenin: I embraced you in a dream—
Inessa: Ran all the way in the cab—
Lenin: And said, I love you.
Inessa: Holding the wind chimes.
Lenin: I have always loved you.
Inessa: You dogmatic dog—
Lenin: Demagogic woman—
Inessa: Autocratic.
Lenin: Dictatorial.
Inessa: Yes.
Lenin: We don't need a parliament—
Inessa: Or a bourgeois democracy.
Lenin: Or any government—
Inessa: Love is absolute.
Lenin: Only the Soviet Workers'-Soldiers', and Farm-Laborers' Deputies.
Inessa: God's the devil in us. On y sois qui mal y pense,
Lenin: Two mushrooms frying in sour cream.

(Shrieking train whistle. MUSIC: O Fortuna, Carmen Burana. first 24 secs. Segue to late evening Finland Station, Petersburg; red flags; bunting; guns Booming; bands play; searchlights sweep the night casting eerie shadows.)

Scene 4

(Climbs a parapet to tumultuous cheers.)
Lenin: Comrades, you have done a miraculous thing. (Cheers.) Pat each other on the back. Frankly, I had begun to doubt this day would ever come in my lifetime. But there you are and here I am, and how GLORIOUS! I confess, I dreaded this moment. I did. I wondered when I stepped from the train would I be taken straight to Peter and Paul? (Crowd: Never!) It may still be the case. Let us hope not. I have only three words: Peace! Land! And Bread! (Voice: "That's four, comrade!" Laughter.) See there? In the "new" Russia we must contend with people who know their A, B, C's! (Cheers.) You have re-written history. (Cheers.) Enjoy your glorious triumph. Bask in it. You deserve it. (Cheers.) But . . . the battle is not over, far from it. Do not lose sight of what still needs to be done. (Voice: What's that?) Securing your gains. Tonight when you are sleeping, even at this moment, those you've ousted are not sleeping, but scheming of ways to regain what you have rightfully taken. In fact, they've already wormed their way back. O, yes, some are already in place—(Voice: Who? Where?)—The bourgeois foot of the Temporary Government is already in the door, their greedy paws already in your pocket. Keep vigil, comrades! Tonight we say to the world of whore mongering capitalists-imperialist-autocrats, to a decadent bourgeoisie, and a shameless corporate elite . . . now it's our turn to dance. *Business as usual is over! Oblige us with your absence. Peace! Land! Bread! Free-dom!*
(Cheering; drums; gunfire; waltzing; singing of International.)

End Part One of Trilogy